Potomac Review

Potomac Review

EDITOR
Albert Kapikian

MANAGING EDITOR
Monica Mische

POETRY EDITOR	**FICTION EDITOR**	**NONFICTION EDITOR**
Katherine Smith	Caleb Berer	Viola Clune

ART & DESIGN	**INTERN ADVISOR**
Ash Weaver	Ellen Sullivan

ADMINISTRATIVE ASSISTANT/WEBMASTER
Om B. Rusten

ASSOCIATE EDITORS

Diane Bosser	Robert Giron	Edwin McCleskey
Conrad Berger	Heather Levine	David Saitzeff
Theron Coleman	Michael LeBlanc	Jessie Seigel
Hieu Duong	Kateema Lee	Ellen Sullivan
Courtney Ford	David Lott	Marianne Szlyk
	Mike Maggio	

INTERNS
Alana McCarthy Light and Yael Fishman

Potomac Review is a journal of fiction, poetry, and nonfiction
published by the Paul Peck Humanities Institute at
Montgomery College, Rockville
51 Mannakee Street, Rockville, MD 20850

Potomac Review has been made possible through
the generosity of Montgomery College.

A special thanks to Dean Elizabeth Benton.

Copyright © 2023

For submission guidelines and more information:
www.potomacreview.org

Potomac Review, Inc. is a not-for-profit 501 c(3) corp.
Member, Council of Literary Magazines & Presses
Indexed by the American Humanities Index
ISBN: 979-8-9858154-1-2
ISSN: 1073-1989

SUBSCRIBE TO POTOMAC REVIEW

One year at $24 (2 issues)
Two years at $36 (4 issues)
Sample copy order, $12 (single issue)

Table of Contents

EDITOR'S NOTE
Cadence and Disclosure 1

FICTION

KATHERINE D. STUTZMAN
Sightings 17

CHARLOTTE WYATT
Beacon 23

MEGAN HOWELL
Anita Garcia-Barnes 55

SIMON HOWELLS
Durban 65

LUKE ROLFES
Jenny from Softball Put Piranhas in the Swimming Pool 91

MATT COLBURN
On the Metro 105

WILHELM SITZ
Release 151

NONFICTION

PHILIP JAMES SHAW
for when you'd been ranked by grade 6

WHITNEY LEE
Trust 41

NAOMI WEISS
The Married Man 73

CATHY SHUMAN
    Such Rest 125

POETRY

TONI HOLLAND
    Ribcage as Window 12

SARA RIES DZIEKONSKI
    Diner's Final Chapter 13
    Family Diner's Facelift 15

LEILA FARJAMI
    War is Bluest 20

ANDY FOGLE
    The Boy My Age: Michigan Wilderness (1812) 36

DEREK OTSUJI
    In Doors 38

PETER VERTACNIK
    Ground Level 51

CHRISTINA DAUB
    Plea 52
    The Pounce 53

NATALIE HOMER
    Hallows 62
    Seasonal Maintenance 63

BETH KONKOSKI
    L'attesa (A Mother's Waiting) 69

LINETTE MARIE ALLEN
    You'll need 600 pounds, Crumbcake 70

LIGHTSEY DARST
    This Year of Realizations 88

DEREK MONG
> How to Keep Yourself Awake
> Long after Your Son Sleeps through the Night 89

JOHN HYLAND
> Toward Evening 102

SARATH REDDY
> Twenty-Four Hour Bagel Shop 103

ALEXANDER ETHERIDGE
> Living Will 123

DUSTIN KING
> This Afternoon's Sacrament 146

YVONNE HIGGINS LEACH
> The Ancients 148

NANCY NAOMI CARLSON
> We Weren't So Jewish Then 171
> Dog Star 172

POSTSCRIPT

CALEB BERER
> An Interview with Wilhelm Sitz 174

> Contributors 182

Editor's Note

CADENCE AND DISCLOSURE

Like other literary journals, a literary journal that issues out of a community college issues out of a collaboration between the arts and the humanities, between, that is, writers and editors, those engaged in aesthetic production and those engaged in critical thinking about that aesthetic production. On one side, writers struggle to bring their visions to life, and on the other, editors struggle to articulate what counts as evidence for the rightness of difficult decisions to accept or reject the realizations of those visions. Plato, by banning the poets from his ideal republic, began the face-off between the arts and the humanities, and while in our republic it is the humanities that are discredited, de facto banned, in a literary journal the disciplines are yoked together, and because a community college is a region that reproduces itself in every region of our republic, its aesthetic philosophy must reckon with a special responsibility to speak from its region of open admission. In Henry Adams' *Democracy*, Madeleine Lee says, "Half of our wise men declare that the world is going straight to perdition; the other half that it is fast becoming perfect. Both cannot be right." At a community college there is no principle of sorting, so a literary journal coming out of a community college must find ways that its aesthetic sees beauty and imagination in their reconciliatory role.

The world rendered by literature is both its disclosure and the means, or terms, of its disclosure. Form not only carries content, it *is* content, and the arrangement of the particulars of each line or each sentence not only creates the whole but *is* the whole. Just as literature does not speak except out of the constituency of which it is made, a community college's cadence, its lived experience, is also its disclosure, and therefore resists abstraction. In Henry Adams' America, Maryland was a border state between Massachusetts and Mississippi, but today community colleges sit in between and among these three states, cheek by jowl and adjacent to opposing elites, as well as all parts of the political spectrum, a commons where the conditions necessary for the fostering of human connection are in place. Montgomery College, among the most diverse in the country, brings not only Mississippi and Massachusetts to Maryland, but Mali and Mauritania and Malaysia as well. The cadence of its lived experience is the ground for disclosures in which the present catches up with the past, catches up with times and places when people were included solely by principles of exclusion. Here marginal groups are not spoken for but afforded to speak for themselves.

The writer is once removed from the world the writer is trying to find, and writes, just as the student does, to find what is missing about him or herself, an investigation that begins with a line of resonance, a cadence that establishes the tone of an investigation that to be successful, must be sustained throughout. There is a world within the world of that opening line, a cadence that carries the call of the question, as well as the terms and the means of the disclosure. In Isaac Bashevis Singer's "Gimpel the Fool," Gimpel says, "No doubt the world is an entirely imaginary world, but it is only once removed from the true world." The cadence required of Gimpel is trust and gullibility for the disclosure that it is better to forgive than to engage in retributive justice, but when contrivance, not cadence, governs, the disclosure comes at the beginning, often in a declaration of some kind, a declaration merely personal, and declamatory: "I like this, I don't like that;" "I am this, I am not that." It is a declaration about which we are, of course, expert, so that what follows it are manifold disclosures of the ways we have been misunderstood and maligned, all of us complaining the same way about different things, our cadences the same, shared with the very people we are condemning, unperceivably disclosing how all of us share in the same disorder, the same disease.

We cannot foresee the circumstances our next generations will encounter, but we can equip them with the tools with which they will encounter them. The most important kind of learning is learning how to learn, and our opinions, though immensely valuable to ourselves, nonetheless, in our students' lives, have a limited shelf life, while the skill of critical thinking, not to mention engaging with the other side—learning, that is, in some sense, as well, the capacity for empathy—lasts a lifetime. Here student interns play an important role in the selection of pieces, and if this selection process devolves into merely being asked whether we "like" a piece, whether a particular piece "sparks" something in us, then we are merely reproducing our role as consumers governed by what we find "interesting," or "amazing," those always ready-at-hand, interchangeable descriptors of our hypercommodified culture, of little or no value to understanding the pieces before us. Instead, we ask ourselves to try to articulate both a piece's disclosure and the means, or terms, of its disclosure, trying not to conflate aesthetic value with personal preference, but asking ourselves to articulate what counts as evidence for that preference so that an aesthetic commons might form.

To have a legislator "reach across the aisle" requires a muscle developed over time—a time when, writ small, a young man or woman performed a spiritual dance that allowed him or her to see the value in an opposing or mysterious way of life or opinion. This kind of reconciliatory approach can be acquired in the study of the humanities. From American literature, for example, we know that failure with honor, not the pursuit of success at any cost, creates the hero. From American literature we know that we need to be more afraid of our own anger than others' hate. From American literature we know that when care is selective, when care is given to one group, but not another, there is no real care—the call for community implicit in our experiment of self-governance, the care and feeding of the public square implicit in it, is lost. It is in the very nature of disclosures governed by cadence that assertions of reality are grounded in and governed by concern for community. Poems, for example, build on themselves, and that is how they are progressive, by making themselves relevant not only to what's happening now, and what's to come, but also to what came before.

In American literature, we discover that what we are hiding from ourselves is also what the country has been hiding from itself, stories and poems not meant to validate or confirm one's own identity, but *others'* identity. In Brigit Pegeen Kelly's "Song," this disclosure comes on the terms of its cadence:

> Listen: there was a goat's head hanging by ropes in a tree.
> All night it hung there and sang. And those who heard it
> Felt a hurt in their hearts and thought they were hearing
> The song of a night bird. They sat up in their beds, and then
> They lay back down again. In the night wind, the goat's head
> Swayed back and forth, and from far off it shone faintly
> The way the moonlight shone on the train track miles away
> Beside which the goat's headless body lay. Some boys
> Had hacked its head off. It was harder work than they had imagined.
> The goat cried like a man and struggled hard. But they
> Finished the job.

The head calls to the body and the body to the head because they long for each other. The goat had belonged to a child. She took care of him, but one morning she could not find him. She went looking but he was gone. What the boys who killed him did not foresee was that the song would not stop, and that it would become their song too:

> The low song a lost boy sings remembering his mother's call.
> Not a cruel song, no, no, not cruel at all. This song
> Is sweet. It is sweet. The heart dies of this sweetness.

In "Song," one might hear the echo of William Faulkner's *Light in August*. After Joe Christmas is killed, his blood, and the memories of the blood he shed, follow his killers:

> They are not to lose it, on whatever peaceful valleys, beside whatever placid and reassuring streams of old age, in the mirroring faces of whatever children they will contemplate old disasters and newer hopes. It will be there, musing, quiet, steadfast, not fading and not particularly threatful, but of itself alone serene, of itself alone

triumphant. Again from the town, deadened a little by the walls, the scream of the siren mounted toward its unbelievable crescendo, passing out of the realm of hearing.

It may or may not be that community colleges are one way to help heal our rift, but in a region of welcome and open admission one can hear both sides calling out to each other, if only in each side's insistent cadence of godly purpose linking itself to the very forces to which it is so vociferously and breathlessly opposed—on one side, everyone disclosing their truths, on the other, few stopping to listen because they too are too busy disclosing theirs. In a literary journal, the arts call for the humanities, the humanities for the arts, since they, too, miss each other. Because the community college is reproduced in almost every county in the country, it is a universal that is reproduced in every particular, a commons where the particular lives in the context of a universal where cadence and disclosure are meant to be the same, an aesthetic commons, access to which is governed by the categories of empathy, responsiveness, and receptivity, forms of discernment not based on personal preference but with the potential to include us all.

Philip James Shaw

FOR WHEN YOU'D BEEN RANKED BY GRADE

In traditions of many, chairs are set and left empty for our particular saints called for in our most specific of moments—believed to be obliged to arise to our occasions. I painted my first chair on a cold morning in late 2019. As a pandemic took hold of time, I went on to paint hundreds of paintings of chairs and began writing to each chair as an entry in a record—a place set for a memory, a person, an occurrence. The conversation between the words and ink collide into an indictment of memory: a broken recollection, stacked over and over. *prepositions for elijah* contains twenty collections of words in concert with twenty paintings—as devotions to saints of absence.

for when **you'd been ranked by grade** is the first piece in *prepositions for elijah*. The opening of a man's interrogation into memory, as it began at an end.

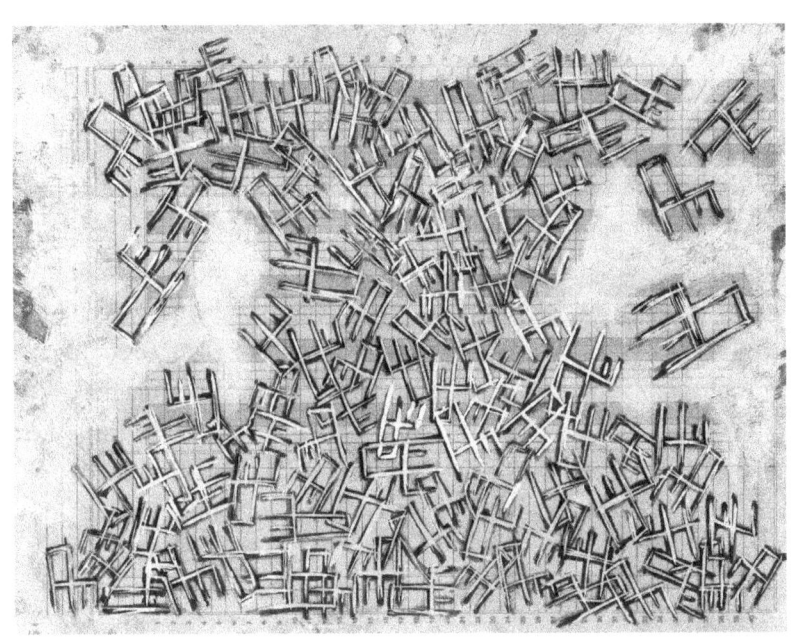

[*prepositions* no. 159 august 5 twenty twenty]

for when **you'd been ranked by grade**

the record provides for how you and i and if there are to be thems of us after us knowing of existence of a record there'd need to be categories in the record we'd all come to call it the record you could argue when you'd argued both for and against a record it was in the record your arguments only another category known for being forgotten from distraction a dust thick category for what'd become months then years now we'd all spent kicking what's owned and felt or what we couldn't any longer know kicked into a field of handfuls we called memories and in the record you'd been told to believe again too many times over and over even when you hadn't believed in decades since times of your touch becoming your lying'est sense after taste the record provided for us categories for shapes of faces even the babies they pinched brows against a powerful sun *more than before* they said before most had remembered by now but you'd also found plenty of photos of squinting children looking into a sun dying from too much sun far back as there'd been photographs *like a sand piper* they'd called wrinkles on a babies brow back then whiskered away on new skin around new eyes how tiny footprints on smooth sand resolves away there'd been a few beaches left as memories of perfection and that'd been the less scary way to say a child's dying than calling them crow's-feet and the footprints in your periphery came early for you dug in even more later and if you *give the baby enough milk lines fade faster* a grandmother would yell about angry babys' faces you'd heard it said before around town from others too no escape from the wind here or sun the damage from when they'd called them *cute crones* babies too little to be burdened with what to try to understand frowned still they'd squint against the light again upon a pitch of paled crowns

as in movies they'd portrayed all the many dead as coral crunching
beneath a villain or heroes booted foot all of what movies stole from
holy texts like flakes of ash in the air the record becomes all those
nights you wanted to remember at the end when you couldn't and
that became the record your loss of memory when all of you became
fine enough to draw into any lung with even a shallowest breath
or misstep the way you'd watch a hero or villain run a fingertip along
an edge of a sharp end set alight unwhitened clouds of what'd been left
of you when you'd set out to search for a category for needing *not-to-
be-known* for forced exhales of you when you'd been one of them
at the end the last of all our deposits of ash all our others you'd seen
rapture fail against gravity over and over no matter when movies or
stories hold a world up to notions of ourselves *here's just one dumb
example* you'd said *take steve austin* six million dollar man an absurd
amount you'd argued back then *they could have saved many more
lives with that amount of money* you'd argued *back then* one afternoon
you'd been going off again over the fence and your neighbor did the
math argued steve was actually under-valued *fucking billion more like
it* is how your neighbor said it *even back then he'd be dead under a
billion* you thought of how all they got for that was only *one extraordinary man* your neighbor said *you know the montage at the
beginning* he worked at the hospital and told you *that's a lot work
they're doing* he calculated the price out loud *cost way more than
millions* is how he said it why not just call him the billion dollar man
you speculated to avoid the controversies of inflation in the seventies
and at night you wondered if that could even be true like jesus
or abraham you'd been torn about both them since your dad gave you
there's a new world coming hal lindsey's comic book fucked you up
it all comes from our same bible your same father had said and you
looked through the back of the head of your thirteen-inch six million
dollar man action figure and pulled back the latex skin on his arm
to see a plastic encased printed facsimile of his robotics a *good american* toy your mother said of *a good white man* your mother said steve
austin was and you could pump a button in his back and he'd lift

a plastic diesel truck engine you'd begged for the bigfoot action figure
played by an andre the giant from the *tee vee show* your mom said *no
he's the brown one* she'd been born putting the article the definite her
expression of distrust of others in her sneer she put *the* in front of all
of her declaratives she hated watching black people on television most
when you loved a fred sandford played by a red foxx and you loved
a staff sergeant kinchloe played by an ivan dixon they called him kinch
in a comedy where nazis were portrayed as bumpkins not even twenty
years after discovery of majdanek holocaust adjacent comedy and you
loved andre the giant rené roussimoff who stood over seven feet
tall who was not a black man even when your mother thought so she
said *he must be* all covered in hair *so big* she said you could wiki in the
record now how acromegaly disordered growth hormones lead to
andre being called an *eighth wonder of the world* in wrestling
at least you showed her on the saturday morning tee vee match
broadcast out of minneapolis pointing to andre circling a middle
eastern threat baked up as heel as our hostages sat put in iran the sheik
had contended for their nation's olympic teams and you said *that's him
that's bigfoot* you said and without having to go many clicks wider
or deeper in the record anyone can bone right up on the sheik or
the giant's friendship with a samuel beckett so you don't feel trashy
and while on the six million dollar man andre had been covered in hair
special *eee fects* your father told your mother agreed with you andre
wasn't black even though he hated monsters said *satan's enemy of
truth* you'd never untied that one but still he tried to make a case
to your mother for an exquisite fifteen-inches of an enemy of american
hero steve austin *he's monstrous* mother said to you and *that iranian
heathen* she turned off your match but to you andre was a god of hair
and of wrestling a giant and even as a toy he didn't do anything
particularly good like steve's toy did but open his chest to show
he too was millions of dollars' worth of monster and man did you ever
pray on your bible to have his toy in your hand and when your mom
went off about him you hid steve fast lest she tied her gift of him to
other strings she liked to do that and blame it on you she'd say *don't*

tie my gift of love to an animal so instead you'd prayed andre might
come through on a training tour in the semis come through your town
until one thursday your father said *i heard about a big man tomorrow
night* your dad called him *a big giant* when he'd bought you tickets to
make you feel better that your mother wouldn't allow a toy of andre
as robotic prehistoric link in your home and he took you to matches
at the vee eff double you hall and said *i think he may be even bigger
than your frenchmen* your father said before there'd been a record easy
to access you wondered at the end how he knew andre was french
dressed up like an abomination on tee vee though mother's right he
said when the main event began that night the giant your father bought
you tickets to see was only a man-boy the flyer photo made him out
to be bigger than he was taken from a low angle instead only
an over-weight boy for his height in starched overalls another farm kid
head shaped like an oboe on that one your father'd said and many
years later you wondered what he knew of oboes since he'd quit his
clarinet drum major history long before you were born never talked
about music and when there hadn't even been a bible left to believe in
you both scratched a hatred that night and some hope into your flesh
to become your belief in giants both of you the record showed because
your ash'd been disturbed made a cloud of you risen to meet up
with all our blood *in all an every lung* scientists came to say *all your
atoms another's atoms* a drop of water in all the oceans in the record
all tiny points you inhabited even some tinier ones you won hadn't
quite made up for giant ones you'd lost and after when nothing was
left of you not a person left among them who couldn't have not known
how to know anything about anyone they wanted to when all there was
to do was search the record where you'd find all of someone expound-
ed upon all recalled could be found right where and when they'd been
if you wanted to look all of where one'd gone what they'd done easy
to find right there in the record except yours you'd managed to become
not a category not to be seen for needing only your shapes left after
your marks coughed up become maps.

Toni Holland

RIBCAGE AS WINDOW

If I could locate   your bones,

I'd hold
      up your ribcage to a firefly

between sunlight

filtering   the doorknob   turning
a shadow traversing the other

way as we discuss *Absalom!*
         Absalom!

       In Marblehead   watching   the ripple

       at the lip

       of sand, eating oysters,

       addressing the difference
       between *a* and *the*,

       I watched your finger
       glide your shirt
       until it reached   the corner

       of your left blue

       eye.   I wanted to linger.

Sara Ries Dziekonski

DINER'S FINAL CHAPTER

He disliked bars and bodegas.
A clean, well-lighted cafe was a very different thing.
—Ernest Hemmingway

Careful, this place is old, Dad would say,
when I'd rattle our diner bones from shoving napkins
into holders and slamming their steel doors shut,
or lengthen the splits of the vinyl booths
when I kneel to wipe the windowsills.

Dad's worn-out these days, too,
scrubbing mugs because the dishwasher
slept in again. *Why not put an ad in the paper*,
I say. *That's how you found our diner.*
He shakes his greys and says
Who'll keep it a diner?
Families just aren't the same,
and in this dead area…
He points to the empty lot next door
where the Rainbow Diner once stood.

We have to sell it to the right person
my father always said, but we all know
that could take longer than his lifetime.

>   (You know how before an old person dies
>   you sense it's their final chapter,
>   but you've yet to learn   its thickness)

These days, each time I leave,
I push open   the door   lightly
the way I hug my frail grandmother
each time we say goodbye.

                      (How you can feel bugs on skin
                          from just the thought of them)

My skin slick with grease.
I can bring back my pissed-off skin
if I imagine sizzling bacon,
stainless steel splattered
with the pigs' last words,
my vegetarian stomach bloated
from just one whiff.

I picture the diner: shut down,
only the bones remain,
and we return as floating figures,
and see all the regulars: Onion Eddie, Eggs Bennie Debbie,
Old Fat George, Country Joe, Safety Pin Joe, Security Guard Richard—
as a child I'd stare at his gun.
I swear I could feel the bullets.

I enter, and all the counter customers
swivel their seats around,
and when they see it's me, they say
Where you been hiding, Kid?

FAMILY DINER'S FACELIFT

Antique cans swaddled in greasy garments of time,
boxed with the Norman Rockwells, penny candy jars
I'd Windex on slow afternoons when all the stainless steel
shined. Fresh paint where the gallery of past owners hung high
above the ice cream freezer: gone. *Ghosts*. The grill banished far
from workers' stories that burn in memory of steel mills.
Soups, gravys, and corned beef hash—my father's recipes
remain, his poems, written for 32 years with hard
spatula scrapes behind the counter. Today I request a refill
and stare at string lights where a payphone once rang dreams—
now still.

I went out into the cold again and again.

Katherine D. Stutzman

SIGHTINGS

We watched an orange-crowned warbler, tiny and plain, on a wintry day when he should have been much farther south. The sun was out, but there was snow on the ground and all the puddles were frozen. The warbler was busy in a stand of cattails, hopping and flitting from one stalk to another. We were worried, waiting for the next piece of bad news, but the little bird seemed unconcerned to find himself here—in the wrong climate, at the wrong time of year—as he bustled back and forth among the cattails in the sun.

Another time, I thought I heard footsteps behind me and turned to see if a person were approaching. But it wasn't a person. I saw three white-tailed deer stepping lightly along, heading off in their own direction, the snow crunching under their hooves.

All of the places you went that winter: you disappeared into waiting rooms and medical offices and the hospital. I couldn't go with you. I went out into the cold again and again.

On a bitter cold day when much of the water was frozen, I watched swans, geese, and many types of ducks: ruddy ducks, ring-necked ducks, gadwall, mallards, bufflehead, Northern shovelers, and something that might have been a redhead or a scaup of some kind but was too far away to see clearly. Clustered in a small patch of open water, they made noises as though they were talking among themselves, a private conversation in which I couldn't take part. I stood and watched as some of them slept, some ate, some dove, some preened, some just stood around on the ice. I thought about how, even though this winter is more severe than usual, more severe than they might have expected when they migrated here, it was impossible to tell if they minded, or even if they noticed. They didn't seem to. They went about their ordinary business in the patches of open water between the ice.

I watched a red-tailed hawk eat a rabbit. The hawk stood on the snow three feet in front of me; it used its talons to hold the rabbit in place and its beak to pull and tear. I could see the hawk working, hunching its shoulders to gather its strength. I texted you a picture. "This is incredible," I wrote. "I wish you could be here to watch it with me." I sent it even though I knew you were in the deep basement where you waited for radiation and wouldn't see the text until later. The hawk ate for nearly half an hour. When it was finished, it flew to a tree branch and began cleaning its feet.

Through the window over my desk I watched the female cardinal we'd been seeing for weeks, the one we recognized by the odd feather that stuck straight out over her wing on the right side. Your favorite of our backyard birds. Mrs. C with the Feather. I thought about waking you to see her, but I let you sleep.

I watched an American tree sparrow rummaging for seeds in the downy top of a reed. The reed blew in the wind and the sparrow rode along with it, focused only on his seeds, turning this way and that to get at them: busy, busy. Eventually he stopped for a moment and sat holding on to the stem of the reed, still and upright, with bits of fluff still clinging to his beak.

I will forget much about those months when you were sick: exact dates; the correct order of events; what I did with entire days, even weeks. There will be memories my mind will refuse to hold on to. I will forget things right away, with astonishing speed, before you have even completed your treatment. But even now I remember these sightings, sharp moments of focus when I witnessed these animals entirely occupied in their own lives while I stood still in mine.

At the end of that winter we watched a red fox trotting alone over the snow. We were together, half a mile from the car—a distance you couldn't have covered two weeks ago, but you made it. The fox was the only bright thing in the winter woods. She didn't know we were there; we watched her and saw the moment she noticed us, lifted her head, turned around and went back the way she had come. She glanced at us a few times as she left, but she didn't hurry.

Leila Farjami

WAR IS BLUEST

War is the bluest of all bodies,
bluer than the sky.
It stands amongst its corpses
with its cold front,
its lifeless limbs wedged between
planets and blood,
bullets and bone.

With an outstretched palm,
we touch
this permanent aura,
marred and mangled
by time.

The bluest
is war:
unchanging in color
under blows and devastation,
it never turns black—my heart —
or purple—your skin —
only perpetuates its blueness,
a sea of natural monsters
handing the dismembered over
to lunar tides,
capsized rafts,
and muffled underwater moans.

Motionless bodies
on a desolate shore,
laid out and nameless,
blanketed like sleeping children
on the warm and shifting sand.

It was terrifying and also glamorous to see the rules of the world dissolve.

Charlotte Wyatt

BEACON

I TOLD the authorities almost everything I know. How I met Beth last Friday when she checked into the Oceanside. How Sunday, I gave her a map of the trail to the lighthouse above Glass Beach. That is where they say a jogger found keys to her cabin in the coastal scrub. When the police asked me to describe Elizabeth Guillory-Hicks—missing, presumed deceased—I said, "A head shorter than me. Light hair, freckles, brown eyes. Big doe eyes. Very beautiful." And then, thinking how I must have sounded, I was moved to protect her honor. "Of course, there wasn't anything between us."

The detective was a big guy named Shelby. "Call me Shel," he confided, as if we might be friends. I wondered what he saw when he looked at me. My shoulders, sloped instead of broad; my height, diminished. My skin is pale some places, ruddy and wrinkled others, after almost seventy years of use. My hair is too long and too thin, always mussed by the wind off the water.

I forgave Beth for seeing me as the old man I'm becoming, but I'm still a man. I noticed the way her sweater clung to her body and the snug fit of her jeans. Her laugh was high and girlish and reminded me of the wind chimes hung off every cabin at the Oceanside. I first heard it when she read my nametag at check-in.

"Byron? Like Lord Byron?" she asked.

"Alas, m'lady," I told her, a hand on my heart. "Ma was a romantic."

I said was, but my mother still lives off Roosevelt Avenue in Queens. Beth laughed then, and I didn't correct myself.

Detective Shel says they suspect suicide. I wouldn't have guessed it from my time with Beth. She only seemed lonely, which is not unusual. Once, a pastor stayed at the resort and asked me to join him at his breakfast. All morning, he blabbered on with stories of his ministry, kept up in retirement by listening to strangers who need a friendly ear. I'm no minister, but lonely people like him, desperate people, flock to the ocean like the endless water will give them peace. I understand them in the same way I think of Glass Beach, where the shore is made from sea glass polished smooth. All those sharp edges are forgiven, over time, by the tide.

I go there when I want a break from the resort or when I want to see something beautiful. Most of my time is spent managing the Oceanside. Like our neighbors between Mendocino and Albion, it is a humble property. There is dense headland forest to the east and the cold shore down a sloping boardwalk to the west. Nevertheless, I have been happy to live on the edge of the continent while the owners stick to the bustle of San Francisco. I am content with the quiet here. The passing companionship of resort guests is enough. It is an unusual life, but it suits me.

Which is all to say, I wasn't surprised when Beth returned to my desk Friday evening. I thought she would ask for the name of a local watering hole, somewhere she could go to be among people. But she claimed to have bought too many bottles of wine at some vineyard between here and the airport in Sacramento. Would I like to share a bottle, she asked me. And I thought, why not? Why shouldn't I share the lobby's patio with a pretty woman while the sun sets?

Beth went on about how thrilled she was to have come to California all the way from New Jersey. She had never traveled alone before. She lit up when she talked about it, though the reason was to exorcise the remainders of her marriage. It ended a month before her husband's arrest. He was a minor official of some kind in a prosperous suburb of New York. It made the news back east. I still wonder if Ma saw the story.

"I asked him," Beth said, "to tell me what was going through his head when he picked up the knife." She showed me the stitches in her right forearm where she blocked his attempts to harm her. They had argued for years. Never once had he raised a hand, she said, but there were glimmers. Hints. The way his shoulders twitched when she disagreed with him. A quickness to name-calling. That he had ripped a pillow in two, once, after a fight with his boss.

Perhaps it was selfish of me to ask questions, to make her relive it. She sputtered through her words and I thought she was a little like a woman drowning. My thoughts turned to her rescue. When the sun was gone, I offered her my coat, even stood to help her put it on, but she announced it was late. I was unsure how to end things until she shook my hand with a cold, shy grip, and left.

I worried she was embarrassed and that I might not see her again. But she wandered through the lobby the next night, Saturday, when most guests head off to dinner in pairs. She apologized for leaving as she had the night before. She said I had been gracious to host her and keep her company. Then she paused and I found my gallantry. I asked if I could return Friday night's favor with some wine of my own. The patio was empty, and I can hear the ocean there when the resort is quiet. I thought she was pleased.

By all accounts, Saturday was the last night of her life.

THEY think she jumped from the cliffs just past the lighthouse. A map like the one I gave her was found washed up on the rocks below. It is a dangerous place. You can see the shore go from wading to diving depth at low tide. The water goes from clear to opaque in all of three feet. Where I grew up, I could never have seen such a thing. The only water I knew was brown and murky with all the garbage of New York. Ma says I moved as far as I can within the contiguous forty-eight, but reminders of her, of New York, sometimes wash up like litter. Like the long kelp tendrils splayed across the tidal line, their bulbous ends popped beneath the heels of bold children.

Shel returned Monday with Detective Ramirez, a woman about Beth's age with a strong, compact frame and heavy black hair, slick as the otters in the bay. She searched my cabin. "Procedure," she said. Shel leaned in the doorway, watching, but there isn't much to see. My books, my notebooks. My collection of sea glass. My work clothes and tools.

"You think someone did this to her?" I asked, but they couldn't say. It's an active investigation, they told me. Did I have any ideas, had I seen anyone suspicious? I tried to explain most people I see in the course of a day are, by the nature of my work, strangers.

"You don't sound like a New *Yaw-ka*," Ramirez said as I led them back across the property. We were making small talk by then, and I told her it's been a while since I've gone back. To Shel, she said, "Let's let the gentleman back to his post."

I told her I was happy to help, but the truth is, the day had exhausted me. The Oceanside's owners had been in touch, furious over guests complaining about the police presence. Cabin 7 wanted to leave early and the honeymooners in 2 wanted a refund. And naturally, I felt awful about Beth.

Instead of these things, I told Ramirez, "If anyone comes looking for trouble, they have another thing coming." I flexed a bicep and growled.

Ramirez smiled. She said to Shel, "You believe this guy? A regular knight in shining armor!"

BETH asked me about myself that last night, Saturday, as we watched the sun go down. She wanted to know what it was like to grow up in the city. I told Shel only that we reminisced, which isn't untrue.

In light of her husband's despicable behavior, I couldn't stop thinking about the fall of '70, during my senior year of high school. Selfish of me again, but I also thought maybe it was what she needed to hear. Maybe it could help her to know I also endured something public and ugly, something that felt inescapable at the time.

That July, I told her, followed the chaos of '68 and '69, of Stonewall and the Hard Hat Riots. I have heard this period in Manhattan described as a war zone, like the jungle conflict raging overseas then. My high school friends, Mattie and Freddie, knew we would apply for deferment, but still, needing to apply at all meant we were earmarked for something bigger and more frightening than we could imagine. Freddie was tall and thin as a whip, and Mattie was short and solid as a sidewalk trash bin. I fell somewhere in between. We were unremarkable young men, and some part of us knew it, and resented it. We found ourselves seduced by the sudden flimsiness of safety, order, authority. It was terrifying and also glamourous to see the rules of the world dissolve.

"What a time to have witnessed!" Beth said.

I didn't let on how much that stung, because it might have distracted from my big reveal: that September, I was held on suspicion of crimes committed by the Chelsea Ripper.

I thought she might laugh at the absurdity of it, but she only said, "I've heard of him, I think," and sipped her wine. The sun had just touched the horizon. The soft light of its departure warmed the briny breeze.

Between June and August of that year, four victims had been found, one after another, in Chelsea and the Meat-Packing District. All women. Stabbed, split. Devoured, if you believed the tabloids. A curfew was set and young women followed it to the letter, but there are always exceptions. Molly Olsen was one.

I loved her. Loved her voice, her smell like strawberries and sweat, her hair the deep red of hard candies my mother kept in a bowl for visitors. But loving Molly did not make me special. Not to her, and not from most of the boys in our school. I had known her since first grade, but she didn't notice we both took the Seven each morning to school, or that we shopped at the same market, or used the same branch of the Queens library.

Molly was in my year but had begun to see an older boy. I knew because I saw her with him once on the train platform. When he went to kiss her goodbye, she pouted and turned her head. He slapped her. She fled down the stairs and he boarded the train.

My own father, I explained to Beth, had not been a good man.

"My mother got pregnant very young. This was way upstate. A tiny town. Her parents kicked her out. When my father took her in, he got violent. She ran away to the city by herself, before I was born."

Beth seemed moved to respond to this, but I wasn't finished.

"I have had the advantage of many years to understand what I couldn't at seventeen. I wanted to save Molly because I couldn't go back in time to save my mother. More than that, I wanted to be a better man than my father. A kind of hero."

Beth nodded. She was a good listener.

I followed Molly's boyfriend from car to car and watched every station for his exit. I convinced myself this man was the Ripper and Molly was his next victim. When we emerged in the sunlight of the Village, he seemed to grow more suspicious, more capable of the outrageous violence in the papers. He finally stopped at a pub on the corner of 9th and Astor. Though I was still months from my eighteenth birthday, I stood at my full height, then a whopping six-feet-four, and walked inside. No one stopped me. Having come this far, I prepared to tap the man on his shoulder, and then—I had no idea. I had never been in a fight before. A uniformed policeman entered and I turned to hide my underaged face. The cop claimed a stool next to Molly's fellow and clapped him on the back. I watched for a while, and waited, but they only talked. After an hour, I slunk out like the coward I knew myself to be.

"Did you ever tell her?" Beth asked. "What you almost did?"

I couldn't summon the courage, but another chance came soon after. Class seemed beside the point, what with the goings-on of the world, so Fred and Mattie and I skipped out sometimes. One such afternoon, I led my friends to the bar in question. I described what I witnessed, and what I nearly did. They were proud of me. Fred, who was of age, brought a round of beer to a dark booth in the back. Then another, and a third, until as luck or something else would have it, our wanted man slipped inside with Molly on his arm. They took the only available stools, near the bar's back end. Near us.

"Molly," Freddie called to her in a whisper blurred by ale. "Come 'ere."

I gave him a look, unsure of what he was planning. Molly only glanced at us. Unimpressed, she turned away.

I contented myself to keep an eye on her as Fred announced his newest theory on the Ripper. A police sketch had been printed in the paper that morning. Freddie thought the portrait's grimace matched the late-night cashier at the deli off 111th. I still hadn't ruled out the man on the barstool next to Molly. Whoever he was, the Ripper was our world's chaos on two legs. As likely to look through the eyes of a stranger as through your teacher's, or your classmate's, or the panhandler you saw every evening at your stop.

Freddie called to Molly again. She swiveled to face us. I'm sure my gaze went first to her pale thighs pressed beneath her skirt, but I also noticed the remnants of a black eye on her rosy skin.

Having caught her attention, Fred turned up the theatrics. "Ain't you afraid of the Ripper?" It was past curfew, is what he was saying. He gnashed his teeth for emphasis. "C'mere, Mol. Let us keep you safe." He meant no harm. It was the best way he knew to offer her an escape.

Instead, she made a sour face until her boyfriend took an interest.

"These boys bothering you?" he asked.

"They think you can't keep me safe from the weirdo who's been eating them whores."

She did not speak this way in school. I had a moment to think this was not Molly even though I knew her face so well: the cut of her hair, even the dress she wore in the same sallow green as her eyes. To this day, when I see sea glass this color on the shore, I can't help myself but pick it up to add to the bowl on my bookshelf.

Her man leaned in our direction to take in our faces. He produced a badge from his pocket. Detective William Bruckner. Billy, to her.

"You boys got something to say?" His voice sounded gruff and stupid to me, though to be fair, I already hated him.

I didn't know how to tell Molly everything I felt. That she belonged with me, someone who would cherish her. That I wanted her. But I also understood I could not compel her to choose me, and with this gulf between her desires and mine, and the beer I had guzzled, all I could think to say was, "You should be careful, Molly."

Her expression eased. Her smile became almost tender. For a long second I felt understood, as if she might drift towards our booth to safety.

The moment passed. Her eyes hardened.

"This is the one I was telling you about," she said to Billy. "In the library. On the train." She nodded to herself. "I turn around and there he is."

My face burned. Sweat pooled beneath the hair on my forehead.

Freddie elbowed me, and laughed, unbelieving. "This guy?" I was the shy one in our midst, tongue-tied when girls were near. A virgin.

Billy sat up on his stool and squared his shoulders.

"Maybe I'm not the only one," she ventured. "I never seen a girl go with him."

Even as my chest folded into itself, as my mouth dried, I noticed her keen enjoyment of the words and the malice behind them.

By this point in the story, Beth looked uncomfortable. She shifted her weight as I spoke. The fog gave the horizon a muted glow.

"Did you?" she asked. "Follow her around?"

"Not the way you mean."

I was a child then, too. A lovesick boy who meant no harm. But Beth did not see it this way.

"So because she didn't like you, she deserved whatever this boyfriend was doing to her?"

"Of course not," I said, and would have explained it better if she hadn't interrupted.

"You had no idea about her. Or what else might have been going on in her life!"

"I can see more of it now," I conceded. "Molly and her mother were poor, like everyone else in our neighborhood. Billy might have meant security to them. He was older. He had a good job."

Beth looked as if she were going to say something to that, but then she started to cry. I didn't want to embarrass her or press my point. I put a hand on her shoulder. She didn't shake it off.

For a moment, I was lost in a memory of Ma. She is still the kindest person I have ever known. Growing up, she warned me of bullies and brutes, from men like Billy to men like my father. She raised me with reminders to be better than they were, like her gift to me that Christmas. It was a new winter coat, presented while we sat together on our little couch. She spread its thick fabric across our laps and asked me to think about all the people who made its warmth and protection possible: who raised the sheep that grew the wool, who sheared it from their bodies, who spun it, who wove it. Who sewed the pieces together, who boxed it up to ship to New York, who steamed it and hung it on display.

My mother had no illusions about the cruelties of a life. All these lives, she was telling me, made a great ocean of people, each with their own thoughts and hopes and hurts as she or I had. She was shaping me to see the world this way, so I could be a beacon, like she was to me. Someone who guided, and warned, and offered safe harbor like the lighthouse over Glass Beach.

"What happened to Molly?" Beth asked, once she caught her breath.

"Get on home, Molls," Billy said in the bar, never taking his eyes from us. He began to unbutton the cuffs of his shirt.

I watched Molly float through the pub's warm dark into the cool evening. The door swung behind her as tense seconds passed. I don't know how many—one, less than one, a hundred—then Mattie and Fred bolted. Before I could think to follow, Billy caught my shirt. I lunged away and we struggled until I wrenched him off on a corner booth. I barely beat him to the door. I made for the subway at a run.

Ten blocks later, I found the station stairs clogged with people. The trains were delayed. I gulped warm air heavy with sweat and breath, which upset the beer in my otherwise empty stomach. I leaned my cheek against the wall's cold tile until I spotted my friends waving their arms near the platform's downtown edge. I plunged into the crowd and started toward them, and this could have been the end of it. But I looked for her. I couldn't help it. She stood away from Mattie and Freddie, in a swell of tired, huddled people, and I thought of Billy's grip on my shirt, of her bruises, of how I could still save her. I made for Molly, who retreated, of course. I think of her now every time I try to trap something adrift in a tidal pool, like the frightened fish I rescue from high-tide stranding. The closer I came, the more urgently she pulled away.

"You must have terrified her," Beth said. "She thought you were angry after what she said."

But it was urgency I felt, to make Molly understand my intentions, and Billy's unworthiness, and the care she must take for her own sake, and mine.

The crowd gave her more opportunities to shrink and hide but also took her closer to the tracks. I called her name to warn her. I swung my arm out to catch her but could only reach the tail of her braid. She screamed and pulled away, and told me not to touch her. So I let her go. She stumbled backwards over the platform's edge and onto the tracks.

"Was she alright?" Beth asked.

I paused to sip the tea I brewed once the wine ran out. By then, the sun was long down.

"Her back broke in two places," I told Beth. "Molly was paralyzed, but she lived."

I waited for Beth to reply but she didn't speak.

"I brought flowers to the hospital. I was never allowed in her room. I left groceries at her mother's door every week until I went away to college. Mrs. Olsen hated me, but she didn't refuse."

Beth set her cup on the table between us.

"Is Molly still alive?" she asked.

"I couldn't bear it, Beth," I told her. "I had to walk away. They were all better off without me. I went to school upstate," I said, and paused. I was unsure how to explain the slow ebb of my life from New York to California. The odd-jobs I worked, the women who disappointed me, or who I gave up on. The years receded so quickly, and the truth was, I didn't know a thing about Molly.

Beth laughed then, or made a sound like a laugh. The shadow of one, like the dim shapes cast on the shore by moonlight.

I FLED up the subway stairs to get help. Billy caught me just as I stepped onto the street. He strong-armed me to a patrol car while I tried to tell him she was hurt. He threw me against the back door, the one for criminals, and hit me across the face. The pain stunned me, then ignited an anger I didn't know I possessed. This fury made me feel capable of any crime, any triumph.

"I know that feeling," Beth began.

"Let me finish!" I said. I startled both of us, but I hadn't spoken any of this aloud in so long. I needed to tell the end of it.

I was helpless as I watched an ambulance arrive. The red flicker of its spinning light lit a gurney that disappeared below the sidewalk then returned with Molly on it. I banged on the windows, desperate to learn if she was alright. No one even looked at me.

After what felt like hours, made worse by the petty ache of my bladder after all those rounds in the pub, Billy approached. He slid into the driver's seat and watched the crowd break up, now that there was nothing to see.

"You've put me in a shit position." His voice was quiet and even but I wasn't fooled. "How old are you?"

"Her age," I said, before I could stop myself.

He struck the top of his steering wheel with the flat of one palm. I jumped back in my seat. We sat in silence after that until he took a cigarette from a pack in the dash. It took him several tries to light it. His eyes flicked to the rearview and stayed on me. Smoke billowed and spread along the windshield.

"We're alike, you and me," he said. "Get carried away sometimes." I felt his eyes on my face where he'd hit me. "Right?" He smacked the wheel again, and I hate myself, still, for nodding.

We drove. I don't know for how long. I sat and suffered in the back seat, bracing myself for a real beating. We never made it to the station. Probably because he didn't trust what I would or wouldn't swear to about him and Molly, a minor. Finally, he parked us near a pier. Lights refracted in the water. I watched the reflection distort the bright skyline above it while he rested his forehead on the wheel and wept.

"He must have hated you," Beth said.

Neither of us spoke for a long time. I thought she might leave as she had the night before. I even wanted her to, a little. But she asked about the Ripper.

"He was never caught," I told her, "though a certain kind of person still tries to solve the case." If she had pressed the point, I could have shown her my notebooks, my newspaper clippings.

After Billy was done with his blubbering, he delivered me home. It was nearly sunrise. He told my mother I was out after curfew. That I had been held in suspicion of the Ripper's crimes, but had also been cleared. After he left, my mother asked about Molly. Word spread fast in the neighborhood. I couldn't lie to her and it turned out she couldn't lie to me, because she never looked at me the same way after that.

"You're going to be okay," I told Beth. She looked at me like I had spoken nonsense, so I tried again. "My mother chose an awful man, but got past it. I got past everything that happened with Molly and Billy, and I moved on."

At first, I thought she took my meaning by the way she stared at the dark horizon, at the gentle, endless waves. Then she stood and thanked me for the wine and I stood with her, which seemed polite. She left without saying good night.

Sunday morning, mere hours later, she came to the front desk. She treated me like a stranger, like she had when she checked in. She asked, "Where can I go to sit with a good view of the ocean?"

I told her about Glass Beach, the lighthouse, and the trail above them both. I marked the route on a fresh map from the folded stack I keep behind my desk. Then she was gone.

AFTER the detectives left on Tuesday, I couldn't think what else to do but go to Glass Beach. For hours, I gathered the sharpest shards and threw them as far as I could over the water, where they might be softened and gentled by the waves. My hands were cut to pieces when the marine cover returned in late afternoon to tuck the cliffs to sleep.

I was thinking of Beth when Detective Shel emerged from the tall grasses that cover the path to the parking lot. He jogged toward me, calling my name until we were close enough to speak over the roar of wind and water. He told me he had been unable to reach me by phone. I told him the signal doesn't travel well this far out.

"No shit," he said. "Elizabeth Guillory-Hicks!"

It took me a moment to understand he meant Beth.

"She went in the woods and got lost. Her phone was out of range and she might not have made it out if some hikers hadn't found her this morning. She's pretty dehydrated. We got her to the clinic in Mendocino. She's heading back east as soon as they release her. I thought you'd want to know."

He gave me the clinic's address and thanked me for my help in the investigation, then left the way he came. I knew better than to go and see her. I'll make do with my memory of the two nights we shared, Beth in her extremity as the sky turned dark. I'll think of the doomed passion in her eyes and her lovely desperation. I'll think on what could have been if time and circumstances were something other than what they were, just as things might have been different on that subway platform so many years ago. I'll remember Beth the way I think of Molly, just before she fell: beautiful, and afraid, and reaching out for me.

Andy Fogle

THE BOY MY AGE: MICHIGAN WILDERNESS (1812)

Tall, gray-eyed, grave
and bashful, this body still
such a jumble, but my host
lavishes praise
on me—such courage! such
maturity!—all in front
of his guests, after helping
feed the herd I will sell

to American troops.
He has enslaved
a boy my age, who is
not stupid, not bad,
and does me *numerous
little acts of kindness.*
His steady work
is pleasure, for

is not the world work?
The man heaps abuse
upon the boy, profanes both
my fathers. I am twelve
and my father trusts me
to drive cattle 200 miles
from home to Detroit
in winter. I am twelve

when this vision
from my Father
lacerates my mind,
flesh to the bones
of what my parents
preach. I am twelve
when the man beats the boy
with a fireplace shovel,

again and again,
with any weapon
that chances.
Is God not
his Father? Here,
he is fatherless
and motherless, as are
they all. January howls

through his thin clothes
and the walls of the barn
where he sleeps. My body
warm in the Michigan
cabin, the angles
of my face rooting,
I am all on fire
with foretaste and prophecy.

IN DOORS

The dead come back to us in dreams
looking like themselves as they were in life,
not paying us any particular mind
but going about their day's business,
watering a sill flower, stirring a pot
on the stove, lifting and dusting knick-knacks

on a shelf. She's finished with the knick-knacks,
and is humming a catch song about dreams.
Then it is time to put on the pot,
playing the same role she did life
as if the day's business
were the same here as there. She doesn't mind

the routine, as if her mind
were content with dusting of the knick-knacks
that in life had been no one else's business
but her own, the collectibles of dreams
—some imagined other life
she'd almost forgotten like a teapot

on the stove. She removes the pot
from the stove, snaps into her present mind,
rung, as by an alarm, back into life,
as if she'd knocked over the knick-knacks,
having been caught up in dreams.
She busies herself about the business

of the kitchen, where she is all business,
lifts the cover off the bubbling pot,
plumes ghosting like vanished dreams.
She seems a stranger to her own mind,
as she arranges utensils like knick-knacks
puzzling out what, what not, to make of a life.

She considers the sill flower's life in a pot,
and is of two-minds about the day's business,
shuttling between knick-knacks and dreams.

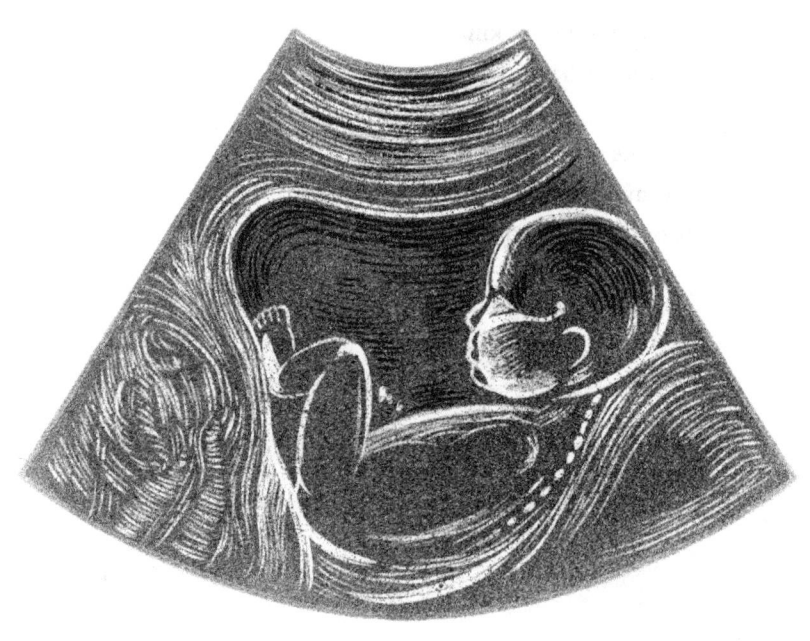

*I met Sabine six years ago when she was
thirty-weeks' pregnant*

TRUST

I MET Sabine six years ago when she was thirty-weeks' pregnant. She had just moved from Oregon to Chicago. I am a high-risk obstetrician and her doctor in Oregon had diagnosed her with a vasa previa—a condition where an umbilical vessel courses through the amniotic membranes over the cervix. Consequently, if she were to labor or her water break, the vessel could tear, and the baby hemorrhage. To avoid this catastrophic outcome, pregnancies like Sabine's are delivered six weeks early by cesarean section. She made an appointment with me to manage her pregnancy.

After Sabine arrived in the office, while I leafed through her chart, the sonographer greeted her in the waiting room and walked with her to an ultrasound suite. From her records, I learned she was a vegetarian, healthy, and this was her first pregnancy. She'd already named her baby Lulu.

After thirty minutes, the sonographer peeked her head around the corner. "Good news, " she said. "No vasa previa."

I examined the pictures of Lulu on my computer screen. The black and white images demonstrated the baby's organs were normal. She was the perfect weight. And the sonographer was correct: there was no blood vessel over Sabine's cervix.

"That's odd," I said as I stood from my chair. "I want to see for myself." Vasa previas don't just disappear.

I walked across a narrow hallway and entered the dark room. Sabine lay on the table. The glow from the ultrasound machine gave her skin a blue tone.

I imaged her cervix from several angles and used color Doppler. The sonographer nodded in affirmation when I failed to find a vasa previa. Instead, I saw a funic presentation. Lulu's umbilical cord floated near

Sabine's cervix in front of her head like a hose drifting in water. In contrast, the blood vessels of a vasa previa are fixed, like pipes in a wall. In a funic presentation, the umbilical cord would likely move before Sabine went into labor and Lulu would be out of danger—we just had to wait.

I flipped on the light then pulled a chair next to Sabine. Her body was strong and lean. Her belly, where Lulu lived, swelled into a smooth mound. Soft monotone fabrics gave her a simple elegance.

"Good news," I said as I sat down. "There is no vasa previa."

She sat up and tucked a lock of long hair behind one hear. Subtle highlights framed her angular face. Her nails were painted a quiet pink, the color of bubble bath.

She put one hand on her belly and gestured toward the image on the ultrasound screen with the other.

"So my other OB was wrong?" she asked.

Reaching a different conclusion than another physician is uncomfortable. One of us was wrong. To a patient like Sabine who is worried about the life of her baby, doubt is food coloring in water. A mere hint alters everything.

"It would be easy to confuse the two conditions," I said.

"What if," she asked, rubbing her belly, "you're wrong?"

If I was wrong, Lulu could die.

Though I was confident in my exam, though there was no vasa previa, I told her to return in two weeks. "We will look again," I said. "Lulu will be ok."

I wanted her to believe her baby girl was safe. I wanted to believe that too.

Two weeks later, Sabine returned for a prenatal visit.

I opened the door to her exam room and asked how she was feeling.

"My doctor in Oregon told me you are wrong," she said. I sat down in a chair and rested my elbows on my knees. "I have to deliver at 34-weeks?"

"Let's look again," I said.

I brought Sabine to an ultrasound room. The images demonstrated Lulu was still a perfect fetus, rolling and stretching in Sabine's abdomen.

I displayed the pictures on a large TV.

"Look," I said, pointing at the screen. "No blood vessel." I pointed at the free-floating umbilical cord. "This is what your OB saw in Oregon. It is not a vasa previa."

To be sure, I worried about the umbilical cord. I worried if it did not move Lulu's head may rest on it and cut off her circulation. But that was an unlikely outcome and not a reason to deliver the pregnancy at thirty-four weeks'.

I wished I had found a vasa previa. Then my assessment would have matched the other obstetrician's and I would not have to contend with Sabine's stress which caused me anxiety. While I trusted my diagnosis, there are no guarantees in pregnancy. It was not that I wanted to be right about the vasa previa. I wanted to right the pregnancy management. I wanted to make the best decisions for Sabine and Lulu.

If something happened, even if unrelated to the vasa previa, I would have wished I'd just delivered Sabine early as her other doctor had planned. After all, I could be have the accurate diagnosis and Lulu could still die. Hell, Sabine could die. Physicians cannot promise an outcome. Ever. Like every doctor, I play the odds. I have evidence and studies. Most of the time, the analytical approach works. But a guarantee? That is not part of my profession. Uncertainty is an uncomfortable reality. It is more uncomfortable when opinions are conflicting and a patient doubts me.

Sabine had to decide. Who had the best plan? The doctor in Oregon or me? If she trusted me and something, anything, went wrong, *what if* would haunt both of us. In some ways, delivering Lulu early presented a solution. That approach would take away everyone's angst. But going against the data and my intellect to appease my gut's discomfort was not a responsible way to practice medicine.

So, I kicked the can. "We can look again at thirty-four weeks," I said.

Before Sabine returned to the clinic, I emailed Ethan, one of my partners and a mentor—someone I trusted. I asked him to review the images. He agreed—no vasa previa. I did not have a reason to subject

Lulu to a preterm delivery. This solidified my science brain and offered some relief to my angsty gut.

When Sabine returned at thirty-four weeks', nothing had changed.

"Lulu is fine," I said to myself as much as to Sabine. I told her the risks of following her other doctor's plan—delivering Lulu six weeks early. The baby would have to go the Neonatal Intensive Care Unit. She could have breathing problems, feeding problems, or jaundice. She may require procedures and be at risk of infection. If we can avoid a preterm delivery, we should.

"I trust you," Sabine said.

"If the umbilical cord does not move, we can do a cesarean section closer to term," I said. "But I think it will move."

Sabine agreed to the plan and we scheduled her prenatal visits for the next three weeks.

Moving a delivery date further in gestation may make clinical sense but it is nerve-wracking. If anything happened in those three weeks, if Sabine got into a car accident, if she tripped and fell, if something unpredictable transpired, I would always wonder, what if she had just stayed in Oregon?

ONE week later, Molly, a hospitalist on Labor and Delivery, paged me. Sabine had been admitted earlier that morning with nausea and vomiting. I dropped my backpack and lunch bag in my office then descended the stairs to the unit. When I arrived in her room, Sabine was wearing a standard-issued beige hospital gown. Her olive skin was tanned from the summer sun. She looked tired but was alert and responsive—even funny.

"I'll never let my husband cook again," she joked. Though she felt terrible, this was the first time I'd seen a lightness to her personality. On the fetal monitor, Lulu's heart rate ticked at a reassuring rate. But earlier in the morning she had variable decelerations where her heart rate slowed for short periods. If the pregnancy were term, these decelerations may have prompted me to deliver Sabine. But Lulu was thirty-five weeks' which was still preterm. Delivery had consequences.

So, I recommended Sabine get intravenous fluid and medications to help with her nausea and we'd keep Lulu on the fetal monitor. That afternoon, once Sabine felt better, Lulu's heart decelerations spaced. I suggested we admit Sabine overnight to watch Lulu and make sure Sabine could eat and drink. Though I was worried about Sabine's health, she was recovering. My concern was Lulu. Maybe watching her all night would provide answers about what to do, how to keep her safe. Should I risk a preterm delivery? Or should I take on the risks of keeping her pregnant? I hoped time would uncover the best choice.

THE next morning, I visited Sabine in her hospital room.

"How are you feeling?" I asked.

"Throwing up eight months pregnant," she said, "is fucking awful."

But her nausea and vomiting had resolved overnight. She was able to sleep.

I scrolled through Lulu's heart-rate tracing: stable and reassuring for several hours.

Sitting in a chair next to Sabine's bed, I asked, "What do you think about going home?"

"What do you think about it?" she replied.

I hoped she would tell me she wanted to stay another night, but she was anxious to be in her own bed. I had no reason to keep in her in the hospital. I worried the umbilical cord near Lulu's head was being kinked, causing the decelerations. But Lulu appeared fine and Sabine felt better. Intravenous fluid would not have fixed complications from a funic presentation. They fix complications from food poisoning. And now mother and baby were well. It made sense for them to go home. My gut was apprehensive but all the data said it was time for them to leave and my brain trusted the data. As a physician, data and science are the holy grail. So, I honored them.

"I have no reason to keep you here," I said.

Dust sparkled in the sunlight that spilled through her window.

"That's great," Sabine said. "I'll call my husband."

I've seen countless pregnant women with a stomach bug. After I sent them home, I did not think about them. But I felt anxious about Sabine. So, I asked her to return to the office Monday as the first appointment of the day. I needed to be reassured. I wanted to be certain Lulu was ok. I worried all weekend.

WHEN Sabine arrived to at the clinic, I waved as she walked into the exam room.

"Feeling better?" I asked.

She gave me a thumbs up.

I worked on charts at a computer outside her exam room while a nurse put Lulu on a fetal monitor. Inside the room, I could hear her searching for a heartbeat. A fetus's heartrate on the monitor sounds like a galloping horse. When we cannot find it, it sounds like radio static. Inside the room was static.

"Fuck," I thought.

The only definitive way to confirm a baby is alive or dead is to use an ultrasound to view its heart.

I hurried down the hall and grabbed the portable ultrasound. Then I pushed the machine toward Sabine's exam room. I hoped my instincts were wrong, hoped when I returned I'd hear the gallop of Lulu's heartbeat, hoped I'd be relieved. But once I arrived at the door—static.

I knocked.

"Good morning," I said avoiding eye contact with Sabine. I pushed the machine to her bed.

"Quit searching for the baby," I told the nurse as I bent over to push the plug into the outlet. I stood and stepped next to Sabine pulling the ultrasound machine closer, still avoiding eye contact.

I turned on the screen, squeezed blue gel across Sabine's abdomen, and placed the probe on her skin. Lulu's head was a bright oval. I scanned toward her torso. I saw her ribs and diaphragm. In the middle of the screen, her heart rested inside her tiny chest. I waited and prayed I'd see it beat. But it didn't. I turned the probe right, then left. Stillness. I put on color Doppler. No flow, no movement.

I watched the screen longer than necessary hoping I'd witness a hint of life. The muscles in my arms and neck tensed. I felt hot. I did not want to acknowledge the truth for myself. I did not know how to share this reality with Sabine. I wanted to pretend all was fine. But there was no choice.

I put my hand on her shoulder. Her pink sweater was soft—her arm, small.

"I am sorry," I said.

I pointed at the picture of Lulu's still heart on the ultrasound machine. "Her heart is not beating."

Sabine grabbed my wrist, her eyes wide, voice frantic. "I don't understand," she said.

"Your baby is dead, Sabine," I said.

The sound of a mother who learns of the death of her baby is visceral and primal. It is not a cry or a scream, it is a guttural wail. Even when I am not in the room with a patient, every time I hear that sound, and I know the news a woman has received.

Sabine sat up and gasped like she was emerging from water—coming up for air.

"I don't understand," she said.

"I'm so sorry," I said.

She reached for her purse on the neighboring chair and started searching through it. "I need to call my husband," she said.

"Of course," I said. "I will be right outside."

I walked out of the room pulling the ultrasound machine with me. I closed the door and retreated around the corner. Then I did something I'd never done in this situation. I knelt in the hallway, put my hands on my thighs, and took long breaths trying not to hyperventilate or vomit.

The nurse and then a sonographer found me.

"Are you ok?" The nurse asked.

"The baby is dead," I said.

Did I kill Lulu? Was this my fault? I had to know. I called Ethan.

"Got a minute?" I asked.

"Is this emergent?" He asked. "I am in a meeting."

"I just diagnosed a fetal demise," I said.

I reminded him of Sabine, how other doctors were worried about a vasa previa and recommended an early delivery. I shared that Sabine was admitted. I told him about the decelerations in the fetal heart rate.

He left his meeting and talked through the ultrasound images and Sabine's hospital course. "You did nothing wrong," he said.

"But if I delivered her early, the baby would be alive," I said. "If she had stayed in Oregon, if she had never met me, the baby would be alive."

"The right management of the wrong diagnosis is the wrong management," he said. "Vasa previa was the wrong diagnosis. You had no reason to deliver her early."

I told him Lulu knew she needed to be born early but I did not listen.

"Lulu could not have known what she needed, Whitney. You did the best you could with the information you had. You are so upset," he said. "What can I do?"

"There is nothing anyone can do," I said. I wanted him to fix Lulu. Rationally, I knew that was not possible. But I wanted to tell him to reverse time, re-start Lulu's heart, make me disappear.

"I will call you this evening and check in," he said.

I felt like a caged animal. My instinct was to leave the clinic. I did not want to see Sabine, her husband, or her family.

After twenty minutes, the nurse walked to where I was sitting and put her hand on my shoulder, "Sabine's family is here," she said.

I returned to Sabine's room and sat down on a chair. Her affect was distant and quiet. "My husband is out of town."

A man and woman in the room introduced themselves are as her father and sister.

"What now?" Sabine asked.

I told her we needed to deliver Lulu just as we would do if she were alive. "We can schedule it whenever you want."

"I want this over with now," she said.

I called Labor and Delivery and Molly answered. I worried she judged me for not delivering Sabine earlier. I felt shame about my choices. "Sabine is here with a fetal demise," I said. "She wants to be induced today."

"What happened?" Molly asked.

My response was cold and operational. "Do you have an available bed? I suspect she will need cervical ripening. I will remind her she can get an epidural."

I returned to the room where Sabine's sister and father stood on either side with their arms around her. I told them there was space for her on L&D. Then I offered them something no new mother should have to consider, an autopsy. "It may help us understand what happened to Lulu," I said. "But it is up to you."

"I just need this over," she said.

Then Sabine's sister and father walked her to the Labor and Delivery. The three of them left the clinic holding on to one another. Her husband flew home and met her in the hospital later that afternoon. I cannot imagine his plane ride, drive to the hospital, walk down the hallway toward his wife and dead baby.

I went home, hugged my four children, then failed to sleep that night.

THE next day Molly called me. "Sabine delivered," she said. "Lulu was gorgeous." She explained the baby had no birth defects or typical signs of death in utero — sloughing or macerated tissue. "She must have died just before she got to your office on Monday." Two weeks later, the autopsy report suggested the same thing—Lulu likely lived through the weekend and died hours before Sabine saw me in the office.

The autopsy report confirmed there no vasa previa but Lulu's umbilical cord had kinked. Her body rested on the it and obstructed the circulation to her body. My brain was right about the vasa previa and gut right to not trust my brain. What I had worried about had happened. I wished I had trusted my senses more and my intellect less. I wished Lulu had lived. I knew my choices could have kept her alive.

SABINE returned to my office for two subsequent pregnancies. I was able to deliver both of those babies—beautiful and healthy. When she first returned to my see me, I offered to find her another obstetrician. "I don't want that," she said. "I trust you." I did not understand her response. I still don't.

In medicine, we remember the literature or our last case. I cannot ignore the evidence and rely on exceptional experiences to guide my practice—that would be irresponsible and erratic. I studied facts to learn how to be a doctor and I am obligated to trust those facts. No one would want a surgeon who solely listened to her gut and ignored the science of surgery to perform an appendectomy or a cardiac bypass. The same is true for pregnancy management. Algorithms and evidence are not disposable even if they are fallible.

Every choice I make as a physician carries a consequence—every medication I prescribe, surgery I perform, and delivery I recommend has a potential benefit and risk attached. The outcome is not predictable. I have to weigh the odds of each option. My job is to balance the magnitude and likelihood of the outcomes that wait on either side of a choice.

After Lulu died, I struggled to understand that balance and trust my internal scale. When an outcome is not what I expect, I question the sanctity of the process. I have not yet figured out how to repair that trust except through time and experience. But science is imperfect and there will always be ruptures in the faith I have placed in it. Perhaps one day the absence of an absolute truth will be too much to bear, the stakes of the gamble will feel too great, and I will hang up my white coat.

I have yet to get over the death of Lulu. I made the wrong choice and Sabine lost her daughter. In some ways, the fact she returned to my care offers me peace. In other ways, it allowed me to love her family more and feel a deeper loss for their baby girl. I am always aware that my internal scale has failed, and I know it will again.

Medical students and residents often ask me how I recover from tragic outcomes like the loss of Lulu. "I don't know," I say. "Sometimes you don't."

The names of the patient and other physicians have been changed.

Peter Vertacnik

GROUND LEVEL

On unrelenting cloudless days when nothing's left
to transform overhead, I lie down prone and still

beneath the black walnut's shade, my mind recasting
the lawn instead. It's harder than with cumulus
or stratus; you can't just spot a cow and call it quits.

Allelopathic roots poison the soil, thinning
the turf in places much like drought. But while there are fewer

choices in that culled herd, the sparseness makes grass easier
to observe: one thick, striated shiv slices my gaze,
like a toenail exposed at the edge of a bed…another blade,

flimsy, frays at its end, a shoelace stripped of its aglet…
From afternoon to evening my mind fixes and drifts,

keeping, like my body, the bearings of a child
as I shift from belly to side to elbow, staying longer
than planned, forgetting laundry and dishes, till dew has groomed

our yard haphazardly and wet, disheveled whiskers
chafe my wrists and ankles, making them itch like hives.

Christina Daub

PLEA

Night spirals into a fog of sleep,
the rain's many voices a spell
that blackens trees where birds
tuck in their beaks. We share
this haven, curled in high nests,
far from the cat on her sill.
I am counting beads,
prayers for a better moon.
Your hat hangs on its hook,
too dry. The lights are out.
The owls do not who-who
circling home. Let me not sleep,
but wait up. I am forgetting you.

THE POUNCE

Today it comes on its soft clawed paws, silent
but for the scrolled leaf scrape, wing flap,
caught breath, the trees screaming.

Today is the day all the furniture you shoved
against the door won't keep it from slipping
in to rub your calves, circling.

There is no tomorrow, only the terrible opening
to what you knew was coming, the flash
of fangs, the pounce, the triumphant

trot away. And afterwards, death purring,
the only sign a telltale feather—his ring you wear
around your neck—and the wet paws, licked clean.

*I didn't want to turn to goop. I didn't want
my body to be broken.*

Megan Howell

ANITA GARCIA-BARNES

THE prettiest girl at St. Catherine's was Anita Garcia-Barnes, the one Pat called difficult. There were others too probably, but I didn't feel like looking through the whole yearbook. It got predictable after a while: pages of acne and milkmaid skin, braces and crooked baby-toothed smiles.

"Where's Anita from?" I asked.

Pat was grading papers next to me in bed. I didn't know high school theater classes had homework, but his did. He'd been teaching stagecraft at Catherine's for two years. "Anita?" he asked. "I think she lives in Hialeah. I don't remember. But her and the black girl I was telling you about never show up on time. It's ridiculous. Sometimes they come when class is half-way through."

"Are they nice?"

"No."

"I was like that too. Difficult." I leaned in to Anita's picture, studying the familiar dimples, green eyes and full lips. "I could pass for her mom. I'm thirty-five and she's like, what? Sixteen? We look related."

"Mhm."

"One of the teen moms at my old school had their son get into all the Ivies. He was on the news and everything."

"Wow."

"It's weird, because my parents were always freaking out about me going down a similar road. Not the Ivy kid's—his mother's. Then the tumors spread everywhere. But I already told you: they make having kids impossible. But sometimes I wonder, like, what if? I mean, I would've wound up sick no matter how many bad decisions I made. Why didn't I have a kid while I still could? They could keep me company if my cancer ever came back. Maybe I'll adopt. I don't know."

Pat nodded. He wasn't listening, but he wasn't grading anymore either. He was doing that thing where he stared into space and swished his mouth. I guessed he was thinking about his divorce. We'd been seeing each other on and off for a few months, and though we were close, he was still in love with his ex-wife, the Australian. Sometimes she sent him pictures of their two-year-old doing cute stuff like wearing a bowl of oatmeal as a hat. They flashed on his phone in the middle of the night when he was asleep, I was awake and she was taking pictures of breakfast half-way around the world.

I felt him on my thigh. His hand was cold, probably from the ice-pack he'd been using to nurse his sprained thumb. I shivered. The cold was part of the reason, but not all of it. I grabbed on to his hairy leg and took in his warmth. He kissed me.

"Pretend I'm Anita," I whispered.

"What?" he asked.

"You're you and I'm Anita. Come on, it'll be fun. I'm bored."

"Meredith, that's fucked." He pulled away. Hypocrite. I'd seen the porn he watched. Stepmother stuff, a real Freudian nightmare. We couldn't stop laughing when the old lady two-doors down bent down into the washer.

"What?" I said, laughing.

His frown lines deepened. I kept wondering what was wrong, didn't he get the joke? Because I didn't know that I was joking until now. Or maybe I wasn't. I stopped laughing.

"You shouldn't do that kind of thing," he said. "People kill themselves over abuse. It's a parent's worst nightmare."

"I'm not trying to hurt anyone." My voice came out squeaky. I should've said sorry. Either that or tell him about all the messed up experiences I'd had with older people growing up. There were so many of them too: my first boyfriend, and before that my old driving instructor, my sister's friend, a neighborhood boy who'd invited me up into his treehouse where his mother couldn't hear me. "I just want to be someone else," I said. "I'm tired of this."

"Of what? Our relationship?"

I shook my head. "This," I said, slapping my shoulders, chest, legs.

"Oh," he said.

Pat knew what I meant. After the last cancer scare, I'd called him up and asked him how I could make sure my organs went to medical schools for dissection. My parents were hardcore Christians who didn't believe in organ donation. Pat's were lawyers. He said he'd have them look into it, but by the time he got the answer, Dr. Livingston called me to say false alarm—my cancer was still in remission.

"Why be something so messed up when you can pretend to be literally anything?" Pat said. He put all the papers on the messy nightstand.

"So I can't be me at sixteen? I was a stunner then. Big boobs, super skinny. It's rare for a girl to have that and a pretty face too. I almost got kicked out of Miss Christian Beauty for being that way. The people in charge thought having me do the bathing suit portion was hypocritical since the whole point of the pageant was modesty. I had a one-piece like all the other girls, so I couldn't figure out what the problem was."

Pat smiled. His eyes looked sad. He shook his head slowly. No, he mouthed.

"Fine," I said. "I'm Pam Anderson."

He made a face. "Someone else, please. I can't stop associating her with my old roommate, the real odd one back at FSU. He had this huge poster of her. I mean, you should've seen the size of it. It was like Big Brother watching you 24/7."

"Jerry Hall."

"These references keep getting more retro. Are you trying to make me feel ancient?"

I pulled the covers over my head, blocking out his voice (him: "Come on, you can't be serious, Mer"). "I don't know how to make you happy," I said. "Just let me sleep here, and then I'll go home and you never have to see me, and even if you want to, I just won't respond."

"I guess I like you the way you are," he said.

I rolled my eyes.

"Seriously."

"You would've liked me better when I was in my prime."

He sighed. "I like you now."

"Would you have messaged me if my profile pictures weren't touched up? Like if I posted one of me without any hair and all bloated? Or one of me right now?"

"I didn't even know the pictures were altered. Your essence is still there. That's what counts, right?" When I didn't answer, he started touching me again, leaning his mouth towards the crook of my neck and speaking into it. "Right?"

"But wouldn't I be better-looking if I weren't so sick? If the medication hadn't blown me up and I didn't have to get cut up, I'd be…" I didn't know how to finish the sentence. I'd be what? Happier? More loved? Even when I was beautiful, I'd gotten hurt. I think I just wanted to be miserable in a way that made me feel beautiful. "I should probably stop," I said. "I'm being a stereotype. Can't be the washed up woman regretting things." Then, in a low voice, so quiet that even I couldn't hear fully: "You've never called me physically attractive."

"You're perfect the way you are," he said.

"You're such a good actor."

"Not sure if that's a compliment, but I'll take it."

I let myself give into him, hugging him, kissing him, believing his lies. "You should audition for parts again," I told him. "Don't teach forever. Get in contact with your old agent again. Whatever happened to that teen action film you were meeting about?"

"It's been almost twenty years," he said.

"So?"

He laughed through his nose. "So I don't think football-jocks-slash-secret-agents are supposed to be balding."

"What're you talking about? I see a head full of curls." I rubbed the thinned out part of his scalp. In my head, I was Anita flattering him for a good grade. I gave him a fantasy within mine, running my fingers through his salt-and-pepper hair. "So pretty."

"Okay, now you're just pulling my leg."

"Are you sure you don't still go to FSU? Are you a freshman?"

"Come on."

"Sophomore?"

"Meredith, seriously."

"Oh, so you're a senior then. Ready for the real world? I bet you already have the perfect job lined up. Has anyone told you that you should act? I'm sure you get that a lot. You could totally play Prince Charming at Disneyland."

Pat kept laughing until he put his Serious Actor expression on. His eyes lit up. "Did I ever tell you that I was in a hair-care commercial?" he asked "I mean, wait, no—I got the role recently, yesterday actually. It's for a conditioner that's just for men. We're shooting tomorrow on the beach."

"Oh my God! I know a real TV-star. This is unbelievable."

Pat got real excited at that. He told me that he was a junior studying Musical Theater and that he'd been single since his girlfriend back home in German Village, Ohio ended things. He talked a lot about making homecoming court in high school. I couldn't stop focusing on his eyes. They were so pretty. That and also the shape of his face, which was angular in a feminine way. He was probably kind back when people let him be whoever he wanted because of his looks. He didn't seem like the type to bully others just because he could.

"I feel so humbled," he said. "I can't believe I'm talking to the woman who was too hot for Miss Christian Beauty and—wait, where you going babe? We just met. Can I get your number at least?"

"I'll be right back," I said, and went into the walk-in closet.

I was so excited that my body vibrated. My fingers shook and my vision pulsated as I searched for my old clubbing dress, the powder-blue one I'd bought during my last cancer-less semester at Pensacola. I'd meant to give it away, but couldn't part with it completely, only partially, so I'd asked Pat to guard it until I lost twenty pounds.

It didn't fit. The bodice cinched my middle too tight, but I didn't care anymore. Pain felt invigorating when I was having fun. It was just like when me and my girlfriends danced in stilettos until our feet blistered, all of us high and drunk out of our mind.

"I'm back," I said, slinking up against the closet's entrance.

Pat's mouth dropped. His eyes sparkled. "Wow," he kept whispering, which worried me until he said, "I didn't know women could look so good in real life."

I climbed on to the bed. The dress kept squeezing me. I looked in the mirror and saw Anita staring back, big-boobed and baby-skinned. The truth was that I couldn't remember myself from childhood. I didn't like looking at old pictures, so the only memories I had rested in other people. Pat's amusement felt the same as the looks I'd gotten from men when I was young, which made me wonder if they'd secretly found me kind of ignorant too. The dress started hurting me worse. Glittery nylon straps dug into my flesh. I couldn't breathe all the way in.

"We should probably stop," I said.

I started undressing, redressing. I'd come to his house in the same outfit I'd worn the last time I saw him, an angora sweater with jeans, nothing special. He didn't object. Pretending had been enough for him. He often told me how the rush of being on stage or on camera was better than sex.

"Where're you off to now?" he asked.

"Bathroom."

I closed the door behind me. Water spots dotted the medicine cabinet's mirror. There's Anita, I thought. I cupped the air where my breasts had been pre-double mastectomy. My insurance at the new place where I worked would cover part of the cost for reconstructive surgery. The problem was that I didn't want to go under the knife again. Too many bad memories. I had nightmares about people touching me.

The fantasy of Anita played out in my mind, dwindling. I imagined myself, Anita, being passed down a line of people: teachers and neighbors, boyfriends and friends, stepfamilies and flesh-and-blood families and driving instructors who stuck their hands in her shirt. People lined up like they were at Disneyland, pulling down their pants, shorts, skirts. The fantasy grew larger until it popped. I arched my back, making sex-faces, and then I was frowning again. The woman in the mirror judged me.

I closed my eyes and thought back to when I first believed I was going to die. I was seventeen and still religious. In my mind, people's bodies were tin cups and the souls Jell-O stuffed inside, and when the cup broke apart, the Jell-O stayed whole. At first, the soul clung to the past, keeping the shape of the broken cup. But then the sun melted it and it got to go to heaven.

"Are you coming out soon?" Pat asked.

Jell-O souls were something I came up with when I was seven and bored, nothing too deep. But the thought of them terrified me in the hospital. I didn't want to turn to goop. I didn't want my body to be broken.

"Mer?" Pat knocked on the door. "Come on, I need to take a leak real quick."

I ran my finger over the scars on my chest, imagining what I could be now that my tin cup was breaking. I hadn't died yet. I could be anyone. My soul got bigger as it expanded across an endless world, growing thinner. I couldn't stop crying. Poor Anita.

Natalie Homer

HALLOWS

What starts as a pumpkin moon
recedes to just another streetlight
shining on a long, scraped smear
of blood on the highway, the deer
—maybe mercifully—removed.

Premise: the first real chill in the air.
Conclusion: there are some people
you'll never wish good for.

In the middle of the day:
egg drop soup, impossibly golden.

I've read the winter-book
with its periwinkle cover,
its distant timberline,
so many times.
I pull it from the shelf again.

Last month, you left your handful of seashells
behind on the Maryland shoreline.
I took two, self-conscious of even those,
worried I shouldn't take any more from nature
than I had already. Still, I put them,
wet and cold, into my pocket,
hoping they might be talismans
for the year ahead.

SEASONAL MAINTENANCE

I drive by the hill where the blue flowers
have left behind dry ghosts of their former selves.

The little yellow sulphurs—clouded or cloudless,
I can never tell—aren't flickering on the hill yet but will be,

a comforting thought I keep in my pocket
like a found stone, good for skipping.

I pass a man weed-eating around a highway memorial,
the little wooden cross freshened with fake flowers.

Just giving up would be easier, certainly.
We must consider how much is owed.

Someone dragged their finger through dust to write
TRUMP on the back of the semi in front of me.

Ho-hum. At work, I whittle a fruit drop to thin glass
on my tongue, and the windchimes do their best

to sound pretty. For a long time, I didn't know
snakes could find their way into birdhouses.

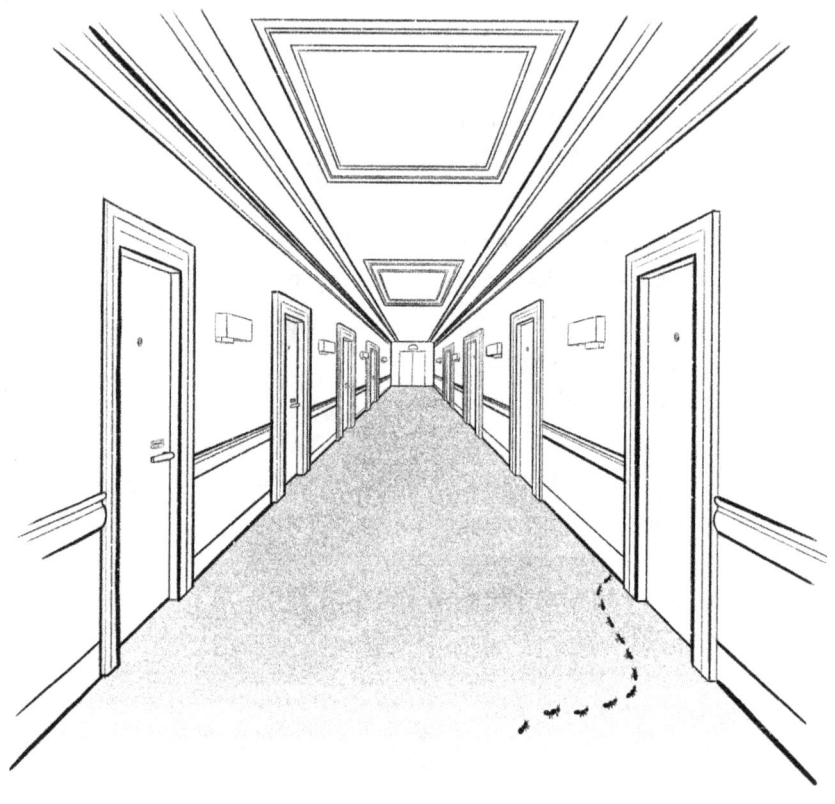

When I closed my eyes I saw lift shafts and corridors and the air was old and slow and moved like tired people on the march.

Simon Howells

DURBAN

I'VE been eight and I hope to be ten. At the weekend we went to a big hotel with a swimming pool. We travelled in our gold Chevrolet and on the way a bird hit our windscreen. My father insisted we should drive back. It took a long time because the motorways go on and on. My mother said only a murderer would care about such a thing. *Maybe it flew off* I said. Then my father found blood in the corner of the window and he wiped until there was no window.

My mother said we had lost time.

Between the hotel and the beach was a road full of cars. Machines are cleverer than people. In the hotel was a big counter that made its man look small. He wore a dark suit and had a parting like a scar. Another man sprayed huge pot plants with water. He spoke to them. My father shrank when he went to the counter. The parting man smiled. He clicked his fingers like a dancer and an old man appeared in blue. He had brass buttons and braiding. The cap was flat on top. The uniform was for a boy. My father said *It's a tradition*.

The lift had scrolls above. The shaft stuck out like a chimney breast. But the lift was cool. It had a carpet and on a stool another blue man. Also old. We went up. There was a dial with a moving hand. The doors opened on a dim corridor. The carpet was so soft I couldn't feel my feet. The corridor was door-lamp-door-lamp the whole way down. Then I noticed numbers on the doors. We were moving, ageing. The porter's breathing was noisy and my father took the suitcase. The porter looked worried. The old man was the only one leaving footprints.

Air was in everything. The cushions, the bed, the glasses, the tables, the chairs. In the corridor you were getting ready for death. Then there was life. I bounced on the mattress. My father patted the porter on the arm and the pat stayed. You can dress yourself in pats. My mother fell onto the bed in a star shape and I jumped on her and when she curled she took me with her and I was in her curl, a smaller curl.

I was born somewhere else and when I was three we came to this country. When we went into our first house I heard crying. I found a ginger kitten in a kitchen cupboard. My parents tell me this never happened. *You must have dreamt it.* But the dream happened and I worry about the kitten.

We were on the twentieth floor. My mother said the swaying was in my head. Birds said *What are you doing up here?* with their eyes. My mother pointed down to a blue puddle that was a swimming pool. I dived out of the window and shrank on the way, disappeared.

I napped in the sky, on air, on things that were and weren't there.

We had to look the part for dinner. The door numbers went down. The corridor felt dry. We went down with the hand in the lift.

I'm good at cutlery. The trick is to hold it loosely, let it play through your hands. I started to tell my father but he got shirty. I am not as prim as I sound. I am a child. I have the ability to think myself down to an ant. There are millions in our garden and if I watch them down I go and suddenly a second is a minute and a minute an hour and an hour is a day.

Because their legs didn't reach the floor I thought they were children. Then I saw their faces. A mother and father with their son all enjoying their meal. My mother told me to eat up.

Later she sat at the dressing table reflected. She said *Sisters*. She was wearing a white dressing-gown. I lay on the bed supported by my elbows. I thank my joints every day. She put on make-up and created and killed herself.

I asked my mother if she had noticed the small people and she touched her hairbrush to her mouth. Can you brush words? She said it was rude to speak about them and I said they couldn't hear us and she said that wasn't the point. I asked *What was the point?* and she used the brush again. When I closed my eyes I saw lift shafts and corridors and the air was old and slow and moved like tired people on the march.

She was dressed in a skirt and blouse. They were shiny. The blouse was white, the skirt was covered in overlapping black and grey leaves. Her eye make-up was pale green. My father was in a navy suit. His shirt collars were large and his side-burns were sharp. My mother stepped into high sandals. All of her was in her arches. My parents met and now my mother caught my father again.

My parents wrote the reception number down. They switched on the television and tucked me up in the double bed. They kissed me. Then they became corridor voices. Then my mother came back with the boy and his parents. The parents were dressed up, the boy was in his pyjamas. Pulling out blankets and sheets is like opening an envelope and what sort of letter was he? His mother tucked him up. She went on her toes to kiss him with a mother look. He tutted. Everyone watched. My father was relaxed. I saw it in his wrists. My mother was her eyes which were big and lidless. The mother fished out a bag of sweets. The adults left.

He said *They are my parents*. Fruit-flavoured jellies. We playfought. We went back under the covers. He curled up and I stretched out. I shaped the white blankets between my legs and I was a figure on a tomb. I must have fallen asleep because I woke up. I couldn't feel my feet. They were bandaged. When I got them out from under the sheets I unwrapped the bandages only they went on for layers and layers until there my feet were small as a baby's. I cried on them. I hoped my tears would wake them. Then the hotel was underground and air was soil getting into your eyes and mouth and the corridors were ant runs. Then I woke up properly and the boy was still asleep.

My father took a wrong turn. We found ourselves on a dirt road. The Chevy has bounce and we were thrown about. The car was driving itself. The car slowed in a one-street place. The buildings were made of tin and the verandahs had thick shade some men sat in with their knees up. Other men sat in the sun their hands over their brows. One man took his hand away and thousands of years were in his eyes. Ants use feelers and other senses. The children looked older than the men.

Noise in the corridor. Walls were brushed and hit. Words were tried out. They were tried again. Long sounds, too many vowels. The consonants were given no chance. Low sounds. Rubbed the wrong way the carpet hissed. Female voices flew worried. We stared at the door. Then it moved.

He had lost his knees and elbows. His head couldn't remember its neck. Sounds fell from him I didn't know. He was slumped between my mother and the small father. My father at an angle I'd never seen. My mother's sandals hung from her wrists. The boy's mother was behind. I caught bits of her. My father fell. Blood stained his shirt and one hand was shocked, bruised. My mother spoke. *If there was nothing he'd go for his shadow*. He groaned. The swollen hand lifted itself and swiped. *He can't stay there* she said and the small father lifted my father on to his shoulder.

In the swimming pool the next day I fell off a step into sudden depths. The water came to me but it was skin that slipped and slid over me, that went in my eyes and my mouth. I breathed until I was full. Headless bodies hung in front of me. Then I was fished out.

Beth Konkoski

L'ATTESA
(A MOTHER'S WAITING)

One cannot measure the weight of Waiting
how it sits curled and pulsing on the chest
while the waited-for goes on creating
an agony of the hours compressed
to this one focus point— my feet must pace.
Was that a door, lights turning up the street?
Long past midnight, rational thought erased
by texts unread, a silence so complete
I'm sure that death, and then a carnival
parade of sirens will be heading here.
I count and pray and beg his car to pull
into the driveway, finish this night's fear.
He makes it home. Friday comes to its end.
Tomorrow night I'll wait like this again.

Linette Marie Allen

YOU'LL NEED 600 POUNDS, CRUMBCAKE

You'll need 600 pounds, Crumbcake

of sundry parts to make a single vat of
Mummy. She's classic—brown as the burns

on my backside, brown as my honeycreeper
birthmark. She's *mum* to some, *mumiya*

to others—magical medicine to millions
more. My daughter calls me Mummy.

I haven't seen her in five years. We live
on different continents, nearly

different coasts. Different blood
lines, too. I dislike turkey.

I look like a Mummy; she looks like
a Spaniard. Will she one day crush me

to a paste, apply me to her newborn's bum
to cure her bruises, her bouts of epilepsy, her

blanched blood—
       half-more,
       half-less?

or carry me in a locket around her free
neck—a little pouch of powdered mummy

and rhubarb? Will she teach her Terrible Two
to paint tall frescos with my charming pigment? My

God, my maiden name is Brown. Does that make me
Mummy Brown? My skin is medium-mummy.

My daughter is mixed up; the lads called her "MUMMY—
WHERE'S YOUR MUMMY?" My granddaughter's

first born looks like Disney's Pocahontas,
whatever that is.

This is this / all over again.

I'll never look at that knock-off
Rembrandt on my wall quite the same.

I'll scratch and sniff, press record—
say to the lover who left it behind: *Woman,*

from where doth thou richest browns cometh?

What kind of marriage did she think they had?
Did I really want to know?

Naomi Weiss

THE MARRIED MAN

THERE were, as always, preexisting conditions: I was divorced; he'd been married for years. I was twenty-nine; he was middle-aged. I was a single mother working at home as advertising manager for *Film Comment* magazine; he was a well-known television comedy writer alongside Mel Brooks, Carl Reiner and Woody Allen; his documentaries award winners; his novels made into feature films; his characters played by Hollywood stars.

I barely noticed the confluence of events that swept me along, each step flowing perfectly into the next, starting when my cousin Ruth moved into my two-bedroom apartment in the North East Bronx to attend Columbia University. With Ruth a willing baby sitter, and Manhattan's New School offering a class in Film Writing, I decided to allow myself one free evening from my lively two-year old daughter, and enrolled for the fall semester, hoping to turn the novel I was working on into a screenplay.

After graduating college in the Sixties, a young woman marries her devastatingly handsome boyfriend, two years later she's a divorced single parent. My life up to then.

On the last day of class, I handed my final version in a clear plastic sleeve to Irving Fineman (not his real name), the man who seasoned his lectures with movie gossip and spicy personal tidbits — a senator's wife cupping his private parts beneath a banquet table at the Emmy Awards; ; a late-night TV host catching his wife *in flagrante* in the men's bathroom at the Plaza Hotel.

"At last," he said, reaching out. "I've been waiting for it. Girls were throwing themselves at me left and right and you never said a word. They were mentally undressing me at each lecture and you never cared. "Why are you laughing?" he asked.

I laughed with him, embarrassment by his attention to the quiet girl who sat at the back of the room, trying to ascertain how he became what I aspired to — a successful writer.

"And then you read your outline. What a woman! Sexy. Exciting. A real heroine. I've adored you ever since."

He was Irving being Irving except the classroom was empty, his blue eyes searching mine, his dark beard and moustache more appealing.

He crammed my screenplay into his worn leather briefcase and squeezed the handles shut. Leaving his brown leather coat unbuttoned, the belt hanging, he walked a little too close to me down the hallway. We rode the elevator in silence to the ground floor, and stepped into Manhattan's crowded West Side streets.

"Let me take you to dinner tonight, and make love to you," he said. "We'll get a hotel room. Is that all right?"

This man, whose professional reputation earned him thousands of dollars a week, who dealt with movie moguls and rubbed a lot more than shoulders with starlets, wanted me? I never suspected or hoped that of all the female groupies who surrounded him, I, who was never among them, would be chosen.

Over the years, I've toyed with rearranging things: If my cousin had studied at Penn; if the class had been full; if Irving Fineman hadn't been the teacher, I would never have encountered what I still cherish, even now, as I write.

With his Hollywood savoir faire and charm at odds with his *haimish* open collar shirts and baggy pants, Irving was as gauche as he was debonair. He instructed, never judged our work, his voice manly yet gentle. I recognized in him my klutzy adolescence and innate shyness. Here was a man who wouldn't lord over me like my ex-husband who lectured me on how to roll up a toothpaste tube, required dinner at six, lights out at ten and demanded I wait beside him when he parked our VW beetle until he turned off the twelve toggle switches he had rigged under the dashboard so no one could jump start the engine.

While my life as a single parent veered between emotional meltdowns and uncertain finances, anti-Viet Nam war demonstrations raged across the country, Simon and Garfunkel sang "Bridge Over Troubled Water," Tuesday nights in Irving's class I laughed out loud. Ninety minutes of him each week for three months validated my independence as a woman and restored my confidence as a writer. But joining him for what he had suggested left me momentarily dazed. Uncomfortably flattered. Yet he had asked with such uncommon ease and nonchalance, it sounded so simple. So natural. Practically normal.

During dinner at O'Neil's, with views of Lincoln Center, and Irving Fineman beside me, I planned to drive home to the Bronx, my cousin and motherhood. But once we were outside, he took hold of my hand as if I was already his. I kept my gaze ahead forbidding how the warmth of his flesh connected me to the man everyone adored. Dare I follow his lead minus the questions and considerations I would normally ask myself? By the time we crossed Columbus Avenue dodging automobiles, blaring horns, traffic lights, and zigzagging New Yorkers, an exhilarating rush rendered insignificant where I was headed. Concern for my safety was negligible. With his hand tight to mine, I simply acquiesced.

Schooled in writing courses and being a good student, I had little experience milling around the lobby in one of the city's frequented West Side hotels while the desk clerk asked, "How many days?" and Irving replied, "The millennium."

My husband was my first. Known throughout our high school for his extraordinary good looks, I'd sneak glances at him as we passed in the hallways. He turned up in my senior year's Oral Interpretation of Shakespeare class at Hunter College. Bronx campus. He took it as a lark, three easy credits, he said, played Petruccio to my Kate in *Taming of the Shrew*. We dated and though sex before marriage in those days would have labeled me a slut, I had waited longer than every female I knew. One afternoon with his parents at work, he unlocked the front door to one of the modest houses off Pelham Parkway. I followed him upstairs into his room, and still appreciate that he withdrew something from his dresser drawer to prepare himself, while I, oblivious, stretched out on his bed. Waiting.

But after being divorced almost two years, without a man at my side or any place else, I was unpracticed at feigning nonchalance while

Irving offered his credit card to pay for a hotel room. Glasses clinked from a bar at the far end. Laughter rose, and to the gentle strains of soft jazz, I obsessed about whether to lean on the front counter, as if that were my routine, or stroll beyond stares of strangers imbibing in the lounge. I was a fallen woman. A certain kind of spectacle. A contradiction in terms dressed in brown corduroy jeans, a long-sleeved turtle-neck sweater beneath an orange three-quarter-length coat I had knitted in high school. What was Irving thinking? He had so many others to choose from.

To escape scrutiny, I walked towards the elevators as Irving plodded past, briefcase in hand, his leather coat flapping. On the second floor, he placed the key in the lock. There was a silent pause, a curtain going up, something flighty in my stomach. The room had dim green walls. Beyond a jagged six-foot rip in the window shade, the view was a brick elevator shaft. There was no television, and a queen-size bed. Even before I glimpsed the dark brown spread and considered the ailments I might catch from sitting on it, I couldn't fathom why the desk clerk had put us here and reminded myself never to recommend the place.

Irving, meanwhile, was in the bathroom with the door open washing his hands. Not his hands, actually, only the tips of his fingers, which he placed under the running water, swiped across a bar of soap, rinsed and dried long and purposefully on a towel. That done, he undressed, placed his clothes neatly over a chair, and just like that, a naked, sloped-shouldered, pear-shaped Jewish screenwriter, my classroom teacher, a respected celebrity, stood before me.

Taking my cues from him, I removed my clothes and placed them, not as neatly as his, on another chair. Desperate to cover myself with my arms, with anything, I turned to face him. It was all so incidental, without direction. Me. Naked and on display. I never considered myself pretty, but I had the certainty of a small, smooth, well-proportioned body. I felt the heat tamper to a slight chill. Goose pimples. Just what I needed. Should I walk across the room, refold my coat to escape his view, warm up? I focused on his straight greased-back hair. If I ever got to know him in a different way than I was obviously about to, I would recommend him to

Richard, the head stylist at Vidal Sassoon's Madison Avenue salon who perfected my five-point pixie every few months.

After what seemed like forever, the warm glow in Irving's eyes turned serious, and he led me, without a word, onto the bed and under the covers. His easy, practiced know-how and surprising physical agility, his impassioned whispers — "You're so easy, so free, so beautifully mine"— overcame my reluctance. He was big and luscious and exciting. He could hold his pleasure, or wait for me.

"Go ahead," I told him. "I want you to."

"Okay. Here it is. Here," and he moved gently, crooning low and soft.

Fifteen minutes later he was ready again. After a second time, "Just a few minutes. You'll see. You're so beautiful. So magnificent."

I did as he asked.

"I told you I'd be fast."

"You're a sweet Jew, Irving."

"Am I really?" He looked at me adoringly.

After one dinner and two hours of lovemaking, this virtual stranger, some twenty years my senior, made me feel as if he'd loved me for years.

"What possessed you?" I imagined my mother's reprimand as I walked to my car, as if she had found out, as if I would tell her; tell anyone. Maybe I was possessed. Driving into the late night along the East River, over the Third Avenue bridge across the Bronx to home, all I saw was a person I never knew in a hotel bed, Irving Fineman asleep in her arms, his head on her breast.

With the start of the Spring semester, and Irving teaching more of the same, I became his honorary guest courtesan. I'd slip into class each week, ease into a seat in the last row and partake of his lecture, free of charge. When fawning females surrounded him at the break, he'd nod and catch my smile as I walked past, faint praise for being set adrift with a lavish secret where everything simply occurred, sequestered from the rest of my life.

After class, under the cover of darkness, we'd head to my car and the Bronx where Ruth welcomed us in her flannel granny nightgown. Ten years my junior, with more sexual encounters than I would ever have, she accepted without question what no one in the 12-story building knew. And we would never tell.

The three of us, comfortable on the cushioned sofa, would speak briefly in hushed tones in the semi-darkness while my daughter slept soundly in her room. After Ruth's goodnight, Irving would follow me into my bed where we would make love behind a silently-closed door. Somewhere around 1 a.m., his warmth still on my sheets, I'd wrap a blanket around me and watch from my second-story window, his leather coat open, briefcase in hand, as he plodded into a taxi waiting to take him to Manhattan's West Side, a place he never called "home," as if the married part of his life — a wife, who wrote an entertainment column for *The New York Times*, a son in acting school, a daughter, a dancer — didn't exist.

I was Bette Davis in *Now, Voyager*, Ingrid Bergman in *Intermezzo*, and Marlene Dietrich in practically everything. In portraying their roles, did each wonder, as I did playing mine: Was my lover's wife wounded by her husband's Tuesday nights of indulging his pleasures with me? What kind of marriage did she think they had? Did I really want to know?

When Irving and I weren't together, I solicited ads for *Film Comment* magazine, and cared for my daughter. This child, born with my outgoing personality and the beautiful facial features of the man who quit his job as an insurance adjuster to travel cross-country on a motorcycle, had given me the courage to divorce. She would become who she wanted to be unencumbered by an inflexible, controlling father who would badger her decisions, stand in her way. At night, with Ruth and my child asleep, I'd set my electric typewriter on the kitchen table, the soft tap of the keys echoing through the silent apartment, and work on my novel. My self worth. My future.

IN moments shaped by tenderness and romance, Irving eased me into his world of movie premieres, book launching parties, and exclusive restaurants. Sitting across from one another in a booth in the Algonquin Hotel, where the famous Round Table of the 1920's and those in the know, like us, engaged in artsy late night talk, he passed me a cocktail napkin: *The guy with the red tie who talks loud is Irwin Shaw. Je t'aime. He used to be a good writer before he became rich and famous.*

I passed it back: *The man in the hip black leather jacket smoking a French cigarette is Irving Fineman. Je t'aime aussi.*

Don't think I'm a celebrity hound, but the man in back of you is Vic Tanney's cousin. Et je t'aime <u>plus</u>.

I basked in the occasion: The Algonquin after midnight, the romantic exchange of billet doux when suddenly, as if someone had yanked the chair from beneath me, everything fell away: the elegant service, the celebrities, the piano music. There was only me over acting, plying my high school French in a performance for Irving because that was what he wanted, or needed. Or both.

Like a stage play stripped of scenery, the moment suddenly laid bare how I had freed myself from an inflexible, domineering husband only to placate and obey another very different kind of man. Irving's fame welcomed me, his adoration was unlike anything I had experienced. I loved his joie de vivre, the sex, our time together. I was his best audience, his biggest fan. I laughed so at his banter, he considered returning to comedy writing. Without the slightest thought that it would or should end, after one semester as his student, another as his lover, a married man had become significant to my life, and in my bed, where he'd climax twice, usually three times.

Orgasms with my husband were easy, and though I never considered Irving old, I held back with him, not wanting to know how he would react to me — that way. Besides, how would his wife feel if she knew her husband and I were having orgasms in the Bronx while she slept in Manhattan, their children in the next room? I could give her at least that.

On the last day of the Spring semester, the students suggested a party. Shopping with Irving for wine, then cheese and crackers inside a West Side A&P, our first time together in daylight felt awkward. Aware that he might be recognized by a colleague or neighbor, I kept my gaze downward and stood somewhat apart from him, forestalling our usual touchy-feely temptations.

In class, students added their own goodies to what we had set out, and female groupies grasped their final chances to entice him. During the year he had lost 15 pounds, published a new book, and with the youthful Sassoon hairdo I recommended, a shag with carefree bangs, Irving Fineman was in his prime.

When I reached out for a bottle of wine, one of the students, his name was Lloyd, approached me. "This one is better," he said with gentle authority. I sipped what he offered, and we exchanged self-conscious nothings.

"Who's with my precious? A student of mine, indeed!" Irving's thoughts glared at me from across the room. He wanted the party to be over, to have me in his arms, in my bed. Jealousy or his uncanny foresight of what was to follow between myself and Lloyd infused our lovemaking that night with a desperation. He stayed with me, matching each breath through my orgasm.

The pleasure was mine, but the gift was his. That glory and sense of accomplishment, I could see it on his face. I had fulfilled my allegiance to a man.

"I love you. Say it," he demanded.

"It would be easy for me to love you."

"So do it. Love me terribly, my darling. We're free to do as we wish."

"You're married. You have a family."

"We're here and they're there. It's all a part of life. What's important is that I have you. Your lips, your neck, your delicious skin. Why are you laughing?"

Oh, he was melodramatic, kissing and nuzzling all parts of me. Of course I could love him as he wanted, but there would be no waking up one morning knowing by his scent that he was mine because he never would be. Parallel lines of action, he had taught, were *de rigueur* for a decent film script. But with us, the lover had no chance to usurp the role of the wife. Rather than needling him to forsake choices he had made long ago, it was easier to accept what he offered.

" You give me enough," I told him. "I don't need more."

With his lips in my hair, his arms enfolding me, "*Daienu*," he said softly, the Hebrew word for "enough," repeated after each traditional blessing offered at the Passover Seder. "HE freed us from Egypt. Fed us with manna. Gave us the Sabbath," Irving kissed me after each line. "But with you, I want it all."

I'd laugh with him, remain part of his life, but prevent my feelings for him from seeping out except in allotted parcels which I could retake before I lost control. An audience needs to see and hear what a character experiences, he cautioned students, and I broke that rule, ignoring what he wanted me to feel, refusing what he wanted me to express. Irving longed to rewrite that part, but that part belonged to me.

SUMMER arrived, and Irving was excited to have me spend a week with him in Paris, then two months in Israel to work on a documentary film, he as the writer, me as the script girl. I telephoned European agencies to arrange for babysitters, gathered passport information, considered what to buy, to pack. Efforts so dizzying, they proved indisputably who I was not — someone able to journey with my child, a toddler, and a married man, my lover, to Paris, then Israel. Such an excursion was magical thinking for a sheltered Jewish girl from the Bronx who had returned home from upstate New York after her freshman year so homesick, she graduated from college two city bus-rides away.

Irving left without me, but not a day passed without me hearing from him. He wrote from Paris on a vintage pornographic postcard, the backsides of two naked women standing in the bois de Boulogne, 1925. "*Tu est dans mon sang, sous mon peau.*" He wrote on Air-mail stationery: "You are the most sensational thing that has ever happened to me." He wrote from Israel: "We will always have each other no matter what happens, even if you run off to California to join the flower children and preach free love with Abbie Hoffman and Allen Ginsberg." He wrote about his work: "Albert Memmi will be coming to my hotel for an interview. On the flight over I'd read his *Liberation of the Jew*; my research was slowed by two incompetents but a strong complaint to the Foreign Ministry's top PR man should rectify matters. Christ, I didn't think I'd miss you this much."

He wrote longing for me to write back. "You cannot imagine in a million years how happy receiving your letter made me. All sorts of depressing thoughts struck me as to why you hadn't written. Your warm, wonderful letter, so much like you, removed all doubts and insecurities.

Each word you write, no matter what, is like a glass of Napoleon Brandy turning my head."

Sometimes I'd read selections from his letters to my cousin Ruth. She'd giggle at the thought of receiving similar phrases from her current boyfriend, but I forced myself to see beyond Irving's words. Our separation yielded the perfect anguish required of any well-written film script and he glorified in it. But he needed more than what he wrote on paper to sustain the drama he created in his life. He found it in a former girlfriend who happened to be traveling through Israel. "Agnes looked more beautiful than ever, but seeing her I suddenly realized that I never loved her as much as I love you." The rest of the page was blank.

Explaining his feelings towards Agnes in a love letter to me, no less! Perhaps the distance between us those two long months had changed him. Changed everything. Was he prophesying our denouement? I pondered a surprise ending, but who would write it, the celebrated teacher, or the student back home?

His next letter arrived the following morning: "I have decided to skip a return to Paris and come home in about a week's time. You cannot imagine how much I not only love you, like you, respect you and appreciate you, but also adore you. I will always be yours."

Despite Irving's artfully-chosen words, I felt a need to gain a measure of control, so I inserted a plot twist. Unable to forget the day in class when Lloyd found the courage to ask me out, his brown eyes widening, his nostrils flaring, I would disregard his banal flattery, his childish ogling, the way he would turn to me from his seat when I passed. Before Irving returned, I agreed to a few restaurant and movie dates, and one dull sexual foray in Lloyd's compulsively organized spotlessly clean Greenwich Village studio. He was raised a strict Catholic in Davenport, Iowa, lived in Manhattan and wrote copy for an advertising agency. There was no need for me to confess.

"You deceived me with my own student. I see it in your eyes. For an anti-Semite she gives me up. An anti-Semite, no less! If I said, 'Rabbi' in class, he'd give me the finger. It's true. Why are you laughing?" Irving laughed with me, trying to hide his hurt, testing my reaction, waiting for a denial, which didn't arrive. I would have given up Lloyd's primping and his over-priced French restaurants if Irving told me it mattered. He never did.

A new semester began and while I continued to date Lloyd, Irving had cast a new player from his class, a pimply-faced editor from Brooklyn, married, no children. I'd seen her with him when I joined him one day after class.

"How can you look at her pimples?" I asked.

"I ask her to turn the lights off. And you're right. She's nothing compared to you. Come back."

I did whenever he wanted, but he didn't want me as much, or as often.

What I still remember from those last few times we made love was watching Irving from my bedroom window, his briefcase in hand, his leather coat flapping, a waiting taxi, and a conversation in bed.

" I'm worried about you. You don't joke anymore," I told him.

"Don't be jealous. You know what you mean to me."

"It's not that. Something's not right."

He took my hands in his and looked down at us touching.

"Being a writer is more important to me than anything else in the world."

"I thought women were."

"How can you say that? Without writing, without my work, there's no life."

This surprised me. I had been glib, but truthful.

"I'm afraid."

"Of what?"

"How can I match my earlier successes, two best sellers, a feature film, documentaries. You've read my latest."

It was a soft-covered exposé sold at supermarket checkout stands. The subject was streaking where a person runs stark naked through a huge public event, like a football game. Reading it was embarrassing. His clever insights were watered down, or non-existent, as if he hadn't tried or no longer cared.

A few days after that conversation, a friend, a student in his class, called to tell me Irving had suffered a breakdown. There had been another, years before, she said, after he had languished without work almost two years before the film of his first book went into contract. The family denied it then, withheld the news from the media. This time his breakdown happened at home during dinner, in front of his wife and children. He had grabbed a four-inch steak knife from the table, and jabbed it into his neck. They remanded him to the same fancy upstate mental facility where he had previously mended.

"Only immediate family allowed," she said. That was the extent of information I had regarding Irving Fineman's disappearance from my life during long months of winter.

My days remained essentially unchanged. I worked to build my advertising client base, and focused on motherhood. I took my growing daughter to Woody Allen's *Take the Money and Run*; taught her songs, *When the red red robin comes bob bob bobbin along*, and had her memorize the title and author of picture books I read. Occasionally I dated Lloyd who was delighted to edge his way into whatever time I allowed him. His insistence that I detail the nature of my relationship with Irving served as an antidote for the poor boy's struggle to experience orgasms, the result of childhood warnings if he masturbated. Lusted after as a courtesan! It felt like one of Irving's jokes.

I waited for Irving to call, to see him again, to be in his arms. After three months, the waiting ended.

"I'm home. I want to see you." His voice sounded watered down by what I might never be made privy to.

"I can't, Irving. Not there." I was excited. Shaken. Intimidated.

"There's nothing to worry about, my darling. I'll be alone."

That was it exactly.

Down a silent hallway dimly-lit with wall sconces in the building's top floor, a somewhat stooped man, his pants baggy from weight he had lost, waited at an open door. I wanted to reach out, soothe him, feel his head against my chest, but that was miles from improbable. He stepped aside, allowing me to enter.

In the living room, wall-to-wall floor-to-ceiling bookcases were overflowing. "I've read every one." He waved, haphazardly toward them.

"Come. I'll show you where I write."

A Dundee Orange Marmalade jar filled with pencils, waited beside an electric typewriter on a teak desk in a bedroom. "My next project." He grabbed random pages from a pile beside the jar, let them fall to the floor. He nodded toward a double bed with a dark wood headboard and rumpled blankets, "I haven't had sex with her since before the hospital."

"Sorry," I wanted to say. "I'm so sorry. I never meant to interfere."

I followed him into the kitchen. He opened the refrigerator door, peered in.

"I'd offer you something, but we don't have much." There was a jar of peanut butter and a half-empty bottle of Coke. He turned and walked away embarrassed for allowing an unwitting glance into his family life. His wife's revenge. Her justification for what she could no longer deny: a husband's late nights, his blithe responses, his begrudging presence. Yet the woman who had awakened that morning from their unkempt bed had chosen to remain despite what she knew. My sympathies went to her. Without a word, his wife had informed me that I was far from Irving's only dalliance. "Let's take a walk," he said. On Broadway, I took his elbow thinking he wouldn't notice the curb. At my touch, his arm fell to his side leaving mine to drop away.

"Some new schmuck psychiatrist is taking me off my medication tomorrow. It's like talking to my senile mother. 'Which son are you, Samuel or Irving? Samuel stayed home, ran our dry cleaning business. The other one, the *nudnik*, he ran off, joined the movies.' " Irving was still making me laugh.

We continued a few blocks, then turned back to his building where we said our good-byes. A nod, no touching. We called one another every few days while he visited Cornell Medical Center as an outpatient. I regretted that we might not be together alone, or any other way. Then my friend from his class called again. Irving had a stroke. He was in the apartment. His son found him slumped over his desk.

Once in class, Irving talked about the right to die. He was angry because people couldn't decide their own eventuality. No one took that from him. "Some people would be happier dead because living had become so much torture," he had said. "At least death brings relief, like good sex."

He was 50 years old.

Beneath the high multi-vaulted ceiling inside Manhattan's West Side Chapel, where famous New Yorkers are memorialized before being laid to rest, endless rows of light wood pews set in a gentle curve were occupied mostly by women, Irving's conquests, I guessed. I sat far back feeling small and alone. Like a groupie, I tried to sort out his family from celebrities. *Remember who you were with him*, I told myself, and straightened up. "Your perennial ingénue," I whispered barely moving my lips. "A stranger to your world, accepting what you gave, protecting myself from what could never be. No regrets, Irving."

Yitgadal veyitkadash shemey raba.

Voices reciting the Hebrew prayer for the dead rose in unison.

Our time together amounted to six seasons and one fatal Spring.

THAT Spring after Irving died, I showed my screenplay to a United Artists producer. He optioned it for six months, suggested a director, cast the main roles, but very little was being created about divorced women. Timing was everything. *Alice Doesn't Live Here Anymore*, a post-feminist movie arrived two years later. Four years after that *An Unmarried Woman* was nominated for best screenplay. The producer said I had a fine talent.

IN a top dresser drawer, inside a small worn wicker box, there's a color photo of Irving sitting at a table in a New York City cafe. He's wearing an open-collar shirt, his hair styled in a shag, a glass of red wine in his left hand. Beneath that is a black and white photo of a woman sitting on a rug. She is surrounded by a dollhouse, a hobby horse, a toy cradle, and a two-foot tall Raggedy Ann slouching on a child's chair.

The woman is younger than I remembered. Unequipped to navigate where she landed. Satisfied for knowing how it would end. Confident she had managed the story from the start, a role played by someone created out of what he saw in her.

Hesitant and uncertain, arms at her sides, legs folded directly beneath her, she glances slightly upward at the camera, her eyes pleading yet forgiving, as she reveals herself exactly as he wished her to be: Naked, content and in love.

November 22, 2020, a story on Hollywood's Golden Age of movies ran in *The New York Times*. Seeing his name, I said it aloud, the sound unfamiliar to my lips; the man who told me, "Nothing can ever destroy what you and I have, will always have;" the man who wrote on my screenplay, "Excellent. Could be better than *Diary of a Mad Housewife*, and as good as *Sunday, Bloody Sunday*. December 1, 1971."

Lightsey Darst

THIS YEAR OF REALIZATIONS

This year of realizations.
They fall out of the walls like ancient bones,
thaw from the glacier's husk like the matted fur
of the first woman. I go along picking them up,
a beachcomber after a hurricane.
I pocket drowned women's wedding rings.
Pull the real from the rhythmic waste of the past.
I will do incredible things.
A decade I tossed into the sea.
Is this my life's work? My life. A work.
My life as a plastic. My mold.
I am a forest, a focus, fierce.
Work until ink-soaked paper blackens pants.

Derek Mong

HOW TO KEEP YOURSELF AWAKE LONG AFTER YOUR SON SLEEPS THROUGH THE NIGHT

Think of the kiddo

    cursed to the chasm

when his doctors botched

    one drug's dose:

limbs ungainly,

    sight and hearing

swept into siloes

    swollen with thought.

Now picture his parents—

    pain-vexed, voided—

learning to love

    by wordless touch.

How do you weigh

    the wails they wade through

against his gliding

    toward gulfs unknown?

And what'll they share—

    his sweet-sense savaged—

save this awareness:

    daylight will rally

in peaceable rhythms

    the plants all know.

Jenny seemed unmoved by the chaos she had caused.

Luke Rolfes

JENNY FROM SOFTBALL PUT PIRANHAS IN THE SWIMMING POOL

Our softball coach was bearded and built. He wore sunglasses and a cool fisherman's style, droopy hat. Some of the parents had crushes on him. Our shortstop hit a kill-shot line-drive when he was coaching third base. He jumped at the last second, the ball missing his crotch by mere inches. The parents in the bleachers went crazy, as if that was the most athletic thing they'd seen.

We got slaughtered that game. It was ridiculously hot—normal for summer in Kansas—and nobody cared.

I remember that game, too, because there was a mom and dad who sat behind home plate in camping chairs. Right in the middle of the sunlight and heat. Their daughter was the pitcher for the other team. She had thick arms and short hair. She was good at pitching but not great. Every time their team was on defense the dad would stand and pace the fence line, his left hand smoothing repeatedly the khaki shorts against his thigh, his chin bobbing up and down as if to assure himself that all would be okay. In the fourth inning, the pitcher walked two batters in a row. A loud noise came from the dad. It sounded like the word "No" (or maybe it was "Naw" or maybe "Oh"). Everybody in the stands turned and looked. The pitcher heard it, too. Her face dropped and turned red. But then whatever had overcome her vanished. She adjusted her mask, spit into the dirt, and called for the ball from the catcher—snatching the ball from the air the way big leaguers do when they know they are better than what they just threw. The mom didn't say anything but stared in the dad's direction as if to say, "Really, Todd? You promised you weren't going to do this again." She pointed at him, and then pointed up the hill toward the parking lot. Eventually, the dad walked in the direction she was pointing.

My own mom would come to our games, usually, when she didn't have to work. She never played softball. I am not sure she knew all the rules. Mostly, she rolled the sleeves of her t-shirt into a tank top and scrolled through her phone.

Some of us would have been happy to see Coach Franky take a softball to the nuts. Like that dad who had to go wait in the parking lot, Coach Franky wasn't as good of a guy as everybody thought. He lost his mind when we made big outs, and said terrible things in the heat of the moment. But then he would apologize—Darn it, if I don't let my competitive nature get the best of me! he'd say—and everybody would laugh and think he was a sweetheart again. There were other coaches who were worse, and who said worse things than Coach Franky. But there are always worse people doing worse things.

JENNY, who played first base, had an in-ground pool in her backyard. After hot games we would go for a swim in the shadow of her giant house, which most of us thought was a mansion but, technically, Jenny said, it was a McMansion. Beatrice was there, as always, wearing a floral bikini top and boy-shorts. She was an outfielder only some of the girls liked, with curly, red hair down to the middle of her back. Anyway, when Beatrice came over to swim this time in August, near the end of the season, she was a real asshole to everybody, talking about each girl on the team's bra size and how it was either too big or too small. Beatrice was a C-cup, and that was ideal, she said, and she ran her hands over her flower-covered boobs like isn't-it-great-to-have-this-incredible-rack. Then she laughed and laughed. Jenny was a little heavier than most of the girls on the team, though she was easily the best hitter. She could, with solid contact, launch a ball over the fence. I doubt there's another person in the district our age who can do that in fast-pitch. She could even do it with a wooden bat.

As well, Jenny had body issues. She used to wear a rubber band around her wrist, and she snapped it as hard as she could for every 25 calories she ate over 1000. She'd eat a third slice of pizza, sometimes, and then say she was going to starve herself for the next two days, or that she was going to the bathroom to stick a toothbrush down her throat. I don't know if I believed that she would follow through with these things, but part of me was certain she at least wanted to.

I asked her once, in a van ride to a game, if she thought she had an eating disorder. We were both sitting in the very back. "Look at me," she said, spreading her hands outward across the nylon seat. "How could I?"

It wasn't the extra weight that bothered Jenny. It was the proportion of her figure. Everything was in her hips, thighs, and arms. Nothing in her chest or backside.

So there Beatrice was, going on and on about her tremendous C-cup boobs, her legs dangling into the blue water. She kept patting her breasts like they were two important trophies she had won. Then she giggled and slid into the pool. In the deep end, she floated on her back, C-cups and chin just breaking the surface. The only person in the water.

There was a little shed next to the pool, painted white with yellow sailboats stenciled on the siding. The door of the shed burst open. Jenny appeared, in her gray one-piece, carrying a five-gallon bucket with both hands.

From the chaise lounge, Tammy looked up and said, "What's in the bucket, Jen?"

"Mind your own business," said Jenny.

"Come on. What's in the bucket?"

"I said mind your own damn business."

Whatever was in the bucket sure weighed a lot. Jenny pigeon-stepped to the edge of the pool and set the bucket on the lip. She slowly tipped it. Dirty water poured into the pool, mixing with the chlorinated liquid. In the bubbling cloud of blue and brown beneath the bucket, frantic shadows emerged. The shadows scattered, flitting in ten different directions.

Fish, I realized. Jenny had dumped a bucketful of fish into the swimming pool.

I pulled my toes from the water, staring over at Jenny, who was kneeling on the concrete. Her eyes were fixed on Beatrice, back-floating in the deep end. I think Jenny whispered something under her breath. And I can't be certain this is what she said, but it almost sounded like she said "Feed."

It was fun to win, and we won, mostly. That summer in particular. Jenny, with the big stick, batted cleanup. I played second and led off. Beatrice, obnoxious as she was, played a mean center field. Chasing almost every ball down with her long legs. Coach Franky (wearing his stupid floppy hat and tank tops) charmed all the parents, drank Gatorade Zeroes, and took the credit for our victories. In between games he talked about his love for the dusty heat and the sound of aluminum hitting the tough hide of a softball, the ring of the ball springing off the bats. I ate enough concession stand food that summer to make me swear off walking tacos and Dippin Dots for the rest of my life.

My dad showed up to one of my games in July, and he brought with him his girlfriend, Lindsay, who was nineteen years old—a mere five years older than me and my teammates. Mom, who always sat at the top of the bleachers, arrived late. When she climbed into the stands she saw Dad and Lindsay sitting alongside the third base fence on a blanket. Mom stood on the top bench, shielding her eyes from the sun with her hand. I'm not sure she knew what to do. She appeared confused, like maybe she was at the wrong field. And then she sat down, hugging herself with her arms. She didn't look so good that day, having worn an old v-neck that was stretched out. I don't think she showered. Her hair was tucked underneath a Royals hat that used to be white. She hadn't worn makeup.

I was having a terrible day at the plate. I couldn't touch the ball. And I made two mindless errors in the field. In the fourth inning, Dad, an all-district outfielder in high school, came to the side of the dugout and gave me encouragement. He told me to make sure to follow through with my swings and my throws. He was watching closely. I wasn't going through the entire range of motion. He had grown a goatee since last I'd seen him, and he wore a linen shirt unbuttoned to the middle of his chest.

In the dugout, Beatrice punched my shoulder and asked what was wrong.

I told her it was nothing.

She asked if it had anything to do with my older sister.

"I don't have an older sister."

"That's good," she said. She was chewing bubblegum. "Because I went out to pee last inning and, over by the trees, your dad was sticking his tongue down your older sister's throat. But I guess she's not that, huh."

"Nope."

Beatrice blew a bubble and snapped it. She said, "Dads just do whatever they want. That's kind of their thing. I'm sure your dad and your older sister have done everything."

"I don't care what my dad does."

"Neither do I."

A ping from a bat. We both looked up to see Tammy ground out to short, but the girl playing first base dropped the ball. The ump ruled Tammy safe.

"I can't lose to girls that suck this hard," Beatrice said, gesturing to the team in the field. They wore bright neon uniforms and knee socks, and they spent the entire game doing these obnoxious chants that involved each player's name.

When I came to bat for the third time, Mom's seat in the bleachers was empty. I had no idea where she went. Next to third base, Dad was standing with his fingers threaded through the chain-link. Lindsay was sitting there, cross-legged, looking dumbfounded by the color of the grass or something.

The pitcher on the other team threw smoke. I always struggled with fast pitches. She had muscular arms and a blonde ponytail.

Her first pitch nearly took my head off. I bailed.

"Hang in there," yelled Coach Franky. "Be tough."

The next pitch bounced off the plate. The next was a strike at the knees. The fourth one looked right down the pipe. I started to swing, but then I realized it was spinning toward me.

The ball hit me right in the sternum. I staggered, gasping and dropping to a knee. Lungs and chest on fire. Pain radiating to my shoulders, arms, and jaw.

I felt the umpire's hand on my back. He was asking if I was okay. And then, before I could respond, he was jogging toward the mound.

Beatrice was out of the dugout. She was screaming at the pitcher for the other team.

"You fucking bitch," she said. "You fucking out of control bitch."

Coach Franky was trying to hold back Beatrice. The umpire was trying to eject her. Parents were on their feet. Voices yelling. My mom was somewhere. My dad was somewhere else. My chest hurt, and I knew I was supposed to jog to first base. There were clouds in the sky. Dust in the air.

In opportune moments, Jenny was our best bat. In the championship game of the "Prairie City Hustle" Tournament, she blasted a walk-off over the center field fence. Her gift was an extra gear most of us didn't have, where she could reach back and knock the hell out of something if she had to. Coach Franky said it was the competitive drive inside of her—muscles stuffed with grit and veins filled with ice water—but, really, I think she carried her anger in her swing.

She and Beatrice used to be close friends, and, in previous seasons, inseparable. They were on another lower-tier team, and they both leveled up together. Coach Franky played with my dad a long time ago, and that was how I ended up getting selected to the current squad. The Bees.

We wore yellow and black striped socks. Golden uniforms. We were supposed to buzz around the base paths. Sting the ball with our bats.

Bad blood developed between Jenny and Beatrice. Neither one of them talked about it. They kept an eye on each other, though, even when they were separated. If a person didn't know them, they wouldn't think anything of it. But the two girls were always on opposite sides of the bench or the huddle. They slapped hands and cheered for everybody but each other. They were good at hiding whatever it was between them, but, sometimes, their intentions would slip out. Once, Beatrice threw away a bag of peanuts she had been eating, and I watched Jenny dig it out of the trash. She spent the entire pregame feeling through the bag, trying to find an uncracked shell with a peanut still inside. She seemed desperate to prove something about Beatrice. That she had been wasteful? That she lacked attention to detail? Another time, Jenny tripled off the pitcher who had just struck out Beatrice. Beatrice, standing next to me, said "god damn it" under her breath and threw her batting gloves at the fence.

One of the other girls claimed Beatrice tried to make out with Jenny near the end of last season, and Jenny had turned her down. Or maybe they kissed one night, and they both enjoyed it, but then the next week Jenny had kissed somebody else—a farm boy with braces and a faux hawk who went by some stupid horse name—Colt, or Pony, or Maverick. Another girl said it had nothing to do with them but their parents. Jenny's dad had slept with Beatrice's mom, or they drank too much at a bar in The Plaza, and he ended up feeling Beatrice's mom's breasts in the parking ramp. She asked him to do it. Or he did it without asking. I can't verify any of these things.

In August, we lost in the semis of a tournament we probably should have won. Jenny struck out looking to end the game on a ball that was eighteen inches outside. As usual, Coach Franky went ballistic. In the dugout after the game, he turned over a five-gallon bucket of softballs and sat down on it, facing the bench. Floppy hat in his lap. He didn't say anything.

After a minute or two of uncomfortable silence, he asked, in all seriousness, if we wanted him to quit coaching and find a better way to use his free time. Beatrice laughed.

He looked at her and said, "Shut up. It's not funny."

It wasn't him telling Beatrice to shut up, but it was his face when he said it. He was already a dramatic guy, but his clenched eyebrows and twisted mouth illustrated how fine a thread he was hanging by. There was something about the way he was looking at her that made me anxious.

"I'm sorry," he said after a while. "I want you to win so badly. But I can't. I can't play the game for you."

I didn't hate him. Not really. I found him tiring. His schtick. His insecurities. How he felt that everything he could possibly do to us was for our own good, our growth as people and athletes. The way he pushed players, as if pushing them could lead them to pushing back in the way steel hardens steel, or some other military-bro anthem that people like him rallied around. I didn't look up from my cleats.

After a few minutes of him lecturing and apologizing, he decided we should go down the line and say one thing we were going to work on before next game.

"Beatrice," he said. "You go first. How are you going to be better?"

BLOOD was in the water. Beatrice's blood. She was hollering, insanely loud—like "make the neighbors call the police" loud. One of the fish bit her, she screamed. She had pulled herself up on the side of the pool, and was bleeding on the concrete from her arm. She was hysterical.

The fish in the pool were also hysterical. Swirling and frantic. They couldn't breathe well in the chlorinated water. They would soon be dead.

Jenny seemed unmoved by the chaos she had caused. She stood at the pool's edge with her strong arms folded. The empty bucket between her legs.

The rest of the girls didn't know what to say. There we were with towels wrapped around us staring at each other's faces for answers that weren't there.

"The fuck, Jen?" Kate said finally. "Did you dump piranhas in the pool?"

Jenny didn't say anything.

"They're bullheads," said Tammy. She was on her knees, peering into the blue and watching the fish flash back and forth. Their snubbed snouts surfaced, briefly, and then more laps around their soon-to-be graveyard. I wasn't sure how she could possibly tell what they were through all the motion.

"I'm sorry," yelled Beatrice. She was on her feet, blood running down her arm. "Is that what you want to hear? I'm sorry."

If these words had any effect on Jenny, I couldn't see it.

WHEN Coach Franky asked Beatrice how she was going to be better, she didn't know what to say. He sat there seething (but with his permanently pleasant body language). It made us all antsy because we knew that we would soon be next, and our minds were scrambling for something trivial to suggest for our improvement, like bending deeper at the knees for a grounder, or anticipating the angle of ball on bat, or wanting it more badly, or trying harder, or paying more attention, or giving more of a damn.

"Coach," said Jenny. All of our heads snapped in her direction. "It's not her fault. I struck out. The loss is on me."

Coach Franky stood up. He said, "Bull."

"I take responsibility. I didn't get the job done. You should be yelling at me."

"Are you telling me what to do?"

"No. I don't know."

His eyes burned a hole into Jenny's. I could tell he wanted to continue unloading on Beatrice, but here was another player—his best player—deflecting and upstaging him. Plus, she was still holding her bat, having made the last out of the game. It was resting on her shoulder. He knew what she could do with a bat—how she could reach back and come forward with ferocious anger if she wanted to. If she needed to.

He said, "You are not as good as you think you are, Jen."

"I'll try harder."

"Will you really?"

Jenny glanced over to the other end of the dugout, where Beatrice was sitting with her head down. She said, "I just want to go home. The game's over. We all want to go."

Coach Franky licked his lips and shook his head. He said, in a quiet voice, "My old coach. If he were as upset as I am now, he would have kicked off the team the first of you to speak up. Not me, though. I'm not like him."

And then he put on his floppy hat and left.

We sat in silence. Then, a couple seconds later, we stood, chattering and forgetting about it. Not Jenny, though. She was staring at Beatrice. The center fielder looked up and spread her hands as if to say she had no part in what had just happened.

Jenny's face, which had seconds earlier looked so certain in its conviction, looked devastated.

I DON'T remember the exact ending to the fish story. Beatrice cried, or maybe some of the other girls cried about the fish being in the pool water, and that they were all going to die. Perhaps it was me who cried. Or Jenny. There was a lot of crying. But that's not unusual for a softball team. Every team I've been on has had a moment like that with most of us in tears. Sometimes holding onto ourselves. Sometimes holding each other. Crying has proven to be an important part of a softball season. It's like when the city workers come by with wrenches to drain the fire hydrants in the neighborhood one by one. I don't remember why they do that. Flushing the old water out of the system must be helpful, or maybe they want to prove to the homeowners that the fire hydrants work, and all that water will protect the people from one day burning to death in their houses.

We used a net to retrieve most of the fish. The kind of net with a long pole—for getting bugs and leaves off the surface of the water. The trick of it was that we could only catch the fish when they were almost dead, and too slow to dart away. They gasped in the white mesh when we lifted them out of the chlorine, too defeated to even flop around. Their slimy sides expanded and contracted weakly. It was not a triumphant rescue.

After it was over, no one felt anymore like swimming. Those who lived close, left. The ones who didn't messaged for their rides to pick them up.

The three of us—me, Jenny, and Beatrice—were the last ones left at the pool party. We sat in chaise lounges on the patio, not saying much about what had transpired.

I wondered how many of my teammates I would see again after the summer. The season was nearly finished. We had one or two games remaining. A single practice, maybe. Each year the rosters would turn over. We'd always gain and lose a handful of players.

After a few minutes of staring into the backyards of the other McMansions, Beatrice sighed. She said, "Do you know what would be funny?"

Jenny didn't answer. I said, "What?"

"If we all quit before next season and did something totally different. Like volleyball. Or soccer. Or got jobs at Applebees. We could say we were re-inventing ourselves. Imagine how upset our parents would be, and Coach Franky."

I thought about it for a while, then shook my head and said, "I could never quit."

Jenny said, "Softball is the only thing I'm good at."

Beatrice shrugged. For a moment, she looked about to say something else, but whatever it was, she kept it to herself.

I'd like to say Jenny and Beatrice hugged it out or had some sort of profound moment there on the side of the pool, but I don't know what happened after that. They seemed to both understand that the other had teeth, but they didn't seem to know what to do about it.

My mom's car pulled into the driveway a few minutes later and I walked around the side of the house to meet her. It was late, later in the day than I realized. The sky turning that strange shade of yellow and pink it does on summer days. Mom was listening to music with the windows down. Her hair windblown and unkempt, her face tanned and lined.

I was wearing a yellow t-shirt over my bathing suit, and Mom was also wearing a yellow shirt. I had a strange feeling when my hand touched the door handle that I knew what it was like to be older, to be like her.

She didn't say hello. As she always did, she patted the seat next to her, and started the song over before driving us away.

John Hyland

TOWARD EVENING

Slippery underfoot,
my daughter and I ponder
the far bank when, as if
from dim medieval tapestries,
they step brightly to the brook:
hooves scratch smooth stones,
thin legs cut current; bare
trees arch over them. They slow
in unison, effortlessly
find pictorial-stillness.
They are so near to behold.
Green water purls
about bones so easily
busted by metal,
ground in gravel.
The sun sinks, darkening
the paths. A flicker passes
over us, its yellow
shafts flashing,
vanishing in the bend
below us.

Sarath Reddy

TWENTY- FOUR HOUR BAGEL SHOP

Insomnia leaps from apartment buildings
onto sidewalks, our sole refuge from night
marked by a blinking neon sign.
I join the line wriggling towards the counter
each segment of the worm taking its time,
paralyzed by permutations of bagel and cream cheese.
So excruciating is the choice of last supper.
Barricaded behind the counter, a stout man
in white, plumed with a chef's hat,
hands too enormous to be trusted with baked goods,
wields a blade meant for an animal's throat—
All this for bagels.
He points his knife towards the list suspended above
laments what ran out hours ago,
the menu slow to catch up with reality.
Now inches away, I am ready with my choice—
the everything bagel with plain cream cheese
because I couldn't make a decision,
black coffee because it is the only remedy for what ails
at 3:00 AM. He takes my tired five dollar bill,
makes me complete with a few shiny pennies in return
then moves on to the next.
He cannot keep pace, the line now stretching to the door.
I find the last empty chair in a corner suitable
for a party of one and unwrap the last twenty-four hours,
the coffee still too hot,
morning too close to think of giving up
my table anytime soon.

*"Didn't you leave anything at his apartment?
What about that jacket?"*

Matt Colburn

ON THE METRO

Sunday, July 15, 2007

"Michael, I need you to come by the apartment." It's the congressman. Most weekends, the congressman is in Ohio with his family. He should be out of town, not in D.C. Whatever it is, it's serious.

On the Metro. Red Line to Glenmont, next stop Friendship Heights. Red Line to Glenmont, next stop Tenleytown-AU. Next stop Van Ness-UDC. Next stop, next stop, next stop, next stop. Metro Center, doors opening. Transfer to the Blue Line in the direction of Largo Town Center. Next stop Federal Triangle. Next stop, next stop, next stop. Federal Center SW, doors opening.

A tall man gets on the train.

"How do you get to Reagan Airport?"

His eyes are a greyish blue. His face is unshaven, and he's wearing a baseball cap that's grey in the front and black mesh on the back half.

"How do you get to Reagan Airport?"

Everyone turns away.

"You have to get off this train and get on the one going in the other direction."

His head moves in my direction. He sits in the row closest to the doors, one row between us. Doors closing.

"My mother died last night."

"Oh."

"I have to pick up my brother at the airport."

"You need to get off this train and go to the train going in the other direction."

"I got in last night."

Doors opening. "We should get off here."

He doesn't move. Doors closing.

"My mother died last night."

"If you want to go to the airport, you need to get off this train."

"I don't understand this metro, y'know. I served in Vietnam and I come back, and you expect me to understand this metro."

"I can help you."

"Bless your soul."

"Thank you."

"My mother died last night."

"Oh."

"I served in Vietnam, y'know. I served my country and they leave me on the street, the government! I know what it's like for them out there in Iraq. It's all about oil. Bush and Cheney, they just want oil."

"You're right. It's not right."

"My mother died last night."

"That's awful."

"I have to pick up my brother at the airport."

"Then we need to get off this train and get on one going in the other direction."

"Okay.

I leave the veteran at L'Enfant Plaza and watch as he waves his hands in the air, asking someone how to get to Reagan Airport.

Doors opening. Doors closing.

Capitol South, doors opening.

The congressman gave me a key to his apartment so that I could check up on things on the weekend. But today, he is here, so I knock. There's no kitchen table in the apartment, so he has me sit on the couch across from him. There are old newspapers on the back of the couch, magazines piled up on the coffee table, and clothes strewn across the floor.

The congressman is 50 years old. He is a large man, used to play football. He has a big white smile, short brown hair. He has a big belly and large hands, and he's about six feet tall. He has big ears, big cheeks, and bug eyes that make him look like he's constantly in awe of the world around him. He was a Beta, a fraternity with which I was all too familiar, having attended Kenyon College ten years after him. He was a Blue Dog Democrat from a distinctly red district, elected as part of the blue wave in 2006. The incumbent had decided not to seek reelection after he was connected to the Abramoff scandal, and the voters were suddenly ready to elect a Democrat after 12 years of Republican rule.

"It's one of the interns. I need you to fire her."

"Sir?"

"Her work hasn't been up to snuff. I don't think she's taking this whole thing seriously."

"Sir, we haven't fired an intern…ever. She'll be gone after the summer is—"

"I don't want to wait. I need you to take care of this on Monday."

"What do you want me to tell her?"

"Tell her we're looking for someone who'll take the job more seriously. This is a big opportunity and we don't want someone who just goes to meetings to get free food."

"Right. I don't have a problem with that. But if you want to sell it better, just so this doesn't come back to bite us, I think you're going to need something bigger. All the interns go to get free food. It's not really a fireable offense."

"Find something."

CRYSTAL City, doors opening.

Fingertips put upon curves, upon curves. Caught in a wave, in a wave. Caught. In a bed, like transport.

"How was work last week?" April says.

"Fine."

She laughs. I begin dressing. April is Armenian; she moved to the U.S. when she was four. Her hair is neck-length and has a blue streak on the left side. There's a mole below her right eye and her eyebrows are sharp: thick toward the center of her face and thin as they stretch outward.

"It wasn't anything out of the ordinary last week. Just the guest worker bill. We got a lot of phone calls, so we are going to take a stand against it on Monday. That was it."

"You mean your boss isn't going to support it?"

"No. It's not like we have much choice. If we do support it, we'll just get kicked out of office and then some Republican will come back in and nothing will happen. It's a compromise."

"I'm familiar with the concept. But if you compromise on everything, it isn't a compromise anymore."

"It's not my decision."

"I guess."

"It's not like the bill has much chance anyway." I tie my shoes.

Monday, July 16, 2007

CAPITOL South, doors opening.

7:50 am. The rest of them won't be here for another hour, at least. The congressman is on the floor in the morning, having lunch with a lobbyist at noon, and in committee meetings all afternoon. He doesn't usually stop by the office when he has a packed day, but there is still a chance, especially if he decides to skip committee.

My BlackBerry buzzes. *I need that speech in an hour.*
You'll have it.

"Good morning."

Rachel attends Kenyon. An English professor with whom I stay in touch gave her my contact when she asked him about internships and called me to tell me it would be a mistake not to hire her. I gave her a phone interview and hired her on the spot. The interview was a formality. Rachel has a 4.0 and works as a student assistant to the English department, the admissions office, and the library. She's also a research assistant to my former professor.

Professor Boykin was the only African-American professor in the English Department while I attended, though that's no longer the case. I first encountered him while taking his "Twentieth-Century African-

American Literature and Political Thought." It was during that course that many of my political positions found form. Writers like James Baldwin and Ralph Ellison spoke to me, though they were writing from a perspective I myself had never experienced. I still remember Professor Boykin discussing in class the moment when Ellison's narrator reads for the first time the words of the note he had been carrying in his briefcase while going from office to office looking for work, thinking it was a letter of recommendation.

Professor Boykin's courses provided a healthy alternative to the Political Science Department, which was made up almost entirely of Straussians. I began my undergraduate career thinking I would major in political science but ended up changing to English after my first course with Professor Boykin.

Rachel is also Black. That makes her the only minority on staff, period. Her hair is straight and in a ponytail. Her skin is dark. She is wearing a black pinstriped pantsuit and a white button-down shirt. After I hired Rachel, Professor Boykin told me how important it was for me to be an advocate for Rachel while she worked in the office. "Ruby Bridges didn't end school segregation," he said. "White men with guns protecting her from the mob did."

"Good morning." I go back to typing.

"Do you need me to work on anything this morning?"

"I'll let you know at nine."

"Gotcha." She slips back into the front section of the office.

The congressman's speech is easy enough to write. Just throw in some stuff about "rule of law" and the "legal immigration process."

"I need to talk to you about something." Rachel is standing by the entryway, her hands steadying her as she leans in.

"Can it wait until nine? I'm finishing something for the congressman."

"Sure." She swings back.

The phone rings. Rachel answers. "Right. Can I have your first and last name…Right, I understand…I'll definitely share these thoughts with the congressman…Yes, I understand…I'm writing this all down for the congressman…Yes, I understand…Sure."

I pop into the front of the office. "Listen, Rachel. Forward that call to me. I'll explain later."

I listen to the guy yack about how we should "put them all on a bus and drive them back to Mexico" while reassuring him that the congressman does not support the bill and "agrees with his position against the bill."

A few more touches to the speech before I send it to the congressman and then I begin writing a script for the interns. The press secretary shows up, then the LAs and LD. Then the other interns and Vicky. The LC and the scheduler quit last month, so I'm doing both their jobs as well as my own.

At the entryway, I say, "Quick meeting in the congressman's office, now. Everyone."

I hand them each a sheet as they walk in, then shut the door behind us. "Interns, Vicky, you get any more calls about immigration, follow this. The congressman is going against S.1348 as of today. Any questions?"

I hold the door for everyone. As Rachel exits, she looks me clear in the eyes. I turn my face to the floor.

By lunchtime, the congressman makes his floor speech, which I had already leaked to one of the local TV stations. *The Columbus Dispatch* and *The Cincinnati Enquirer* are both carrying headlines online. The calls start to die down by the afternoon.

I switch the TV to C-SPAN 3 and wait. The hearing has started but the congressman isn't in his seat. I stand up and pace. The congressman sits down, and he disappears as I flash the TV off. As I stand in the entryway between the two offices, I hear Vicky joking with the interns about how our constituents "would be upset if they heard us speaking Spanish to each other." Vicky was a Spanish major and she likes to answer the interns in Spanish whenever they ask her to do something they can do themselves. Today, it's "Puedes imprimir más" when one of the interns asks for copies of a letter to send out.

"Wait, Vicky." Her desk is by the door. "We should write a new immigration response letter and follow up again with all the people who called in last week. Use the script I gave you this morning and draft something for me. I'll look it over and send it back to you."

"Directamente."

When I put my hand on April's leg, it's like someone lit a fire in my stomach. Like shoveling coal in. When I start to dress, April is in the kitchen.

"Want to split a mango? I can't finish the thing myself. I bought this today, after work. Sometimes, I'll go to the supermarket just to buy one mango."

"Sure." I sit down at the table by the window while she cuts the slices.

She brings the mango and splits off a section before passing the dish to me. "I guess you went through with it."

"Not yet."

She tilts her head sideways.

"Oh, yeah. We went through with it."

"I watch the news, you know. You can't fool me."

"Right…No, I know. We went through with it. I thought you'd be busy spaying and neutering or something."

"Not until I finish school." She wags her finger.

"Oh."

Tuesday, July 17, 2007

The congressman calls me into his private office. "Why is she still here?" he asks before I sit down.

"You said to find something. I can't fire her two weeks after something happened, so it has to be something new, right?"

"I thought you might be holding out on me, but I guess you're not that stupid."

"No, sir. I know how things work around here."

I'm on the phone morning to afternoon with different Hispanic organizations, trying to assure them that the congressman is in favor of "comprehensive immigration reform."

"Someone called, asking about a passport."

Rachel is standing in front of my desk.

"When did they call?"

"This morning."

"This morning?"

"Yeah. I didn't want to bother you earlier. You were on the phone."

"Who was it?"

"I wrote it down at my desk, let me go get it."

"Okay, but when you get to your desk, just call me and give it to me. Don't waste time walking back."

"Okay."

After I finish, I walk to Rachel's desk. "Next time that happens, send the call to me right away. We expedite the passport process for anyone who's about to go on vacation.

People buy expensive tickets without planning ahead and expect us to bail them out. And we do. It's urgent, so just make sure I get those calls right away."

"Whatʼs wrong?" April says.

"Nothing. I'm just tired. Long day. I'll be ready tomorrow."

"It's not that. I don't care about that."

"Oh."

"What is it?" She puts her finger on my chest. "What's there?"

I stand up, begin pacing.

"Whenever you're ready."

"No, I can't talk about office things. I'm not really supposed to share what goes on before it comes out."

"Right. Ooo, this must be a juicy one."

I sit back down on the bed. She puts her hand on my shoulder blade.

"The congressman asked me to fire someone."

"Do they deserve to be fired?"

"No."

"Are you going to go through with it?"

"I don't know."

Wednesday, July 18, 2007

FARRAGUT North, doors opening. The street musician. The bucket, pots, pans, trash-can-top drummer. And all the parts in a cart. Gets on the train. A Black man. Dragging his cart on the car and people shooting strange looks. "How do you get to Court House?"

"I don't know, I'm not from here," they say.

"How do you get to Court House?"

"Get off at Metro Center and transfer to the Orange Line," I say. Metro Center, doors opening.

"How do you get to Court House?"

"You missed the transfer station. You have to get off the train and go back in the other direction." He stares at me.

A white man with a full white beard is sitting near him. He's in a striped dress shirt and tie.

"How do you get to Court House?"

The bearded man moves his seat.

"Get off the train now and go over there and get on that train. That will take you back in the other direction."

And he does and, as the train takes off again, he's there on the platform, asking someone how to get to Court House.

THE congressman is in the office, but barely visible. He is in and out of meetings with lobbyists. I greet each one at the door and then talk with them while they wait for their meeting. The others follow suit.

"Hi, I'm Henry Lloyd, I'm the LD."

"I'm Jennifer, I'm one of the LAs."

"Hello, I'm Bill, I'm the press secretary."

Nice to meet you, nice to meet you, nice to meet you. We go by rank, each person taking their turn to make small talk while the guests wait. Vicky comes up too, and the interns, except for Rachel, who is sitting in the corner, at her computer, working on I don't know what.

"I just remembered. You wanted to talk to me about something the other day, right?"

She looks up. "Yes. But not here."

"Okay. I'll step out for lunch now. Wait fifteen minutes, then meet me in the cafeteria."

I order a chicken Caesar salad wrap and take a seat by the door.

Rachel is by the salad bar. I wave her over. She has no tray, no food.

"Have a seat." I slide the chair in her direction with my foot.

Her eyes trace the walls and the ceiling.

I take a bite out of my wrap.

Her eyes meet mine. "I'm not sure how to say this."

"Just say it."

"I'm not even sure what happened, not really…And I don't want you to think I'm lying, because I'm not."

"Whoa, slow down, I didn't—we didn't—no one's saying you're lying. I haven't even heard what you're going to tell me yet."

"It's about Nick."

"You mean the congressman."

She looks to the left, then to the right.

"Yes. I was at his apartment Saturday night."

She tells me the whole story. It is familiar enough. The congressman called her to ask her if she was interested in talking about a long-term position starting next summer, after she graduated. He told her to meet him at his place to discuss her qualifications. He even asked her to bring a copy of her resume. Then when she rang the doorbell, he showed up in a bathrobe. She tried to leave a couple of times, but the congressman assured her this was standard procedure. He always had weekend meetings at his apartment. And he always wore his bathrobe too.

It didn't matter whether the excuses were believable; it only mattered that he said them with his deep baritone voice and toothpaste-commercial-smile. He asked if he could give her a massage and, after a few "No-thank-yous," pulled her jacket off on his own. He kissed her on the neck a couple of times before asking her to come to the bedroom.

"I said, 'It's getting late. My mom is going to be wondering where I am. Maybe we can talk about this on Monday.'" She was bouncing her knee as she told me the story.

"He said, 'No, we can't talk about this on Monday. You embarrassed me.'"

I could picture him slamming the door in her face.

"I just wanted someone to talk to. I know I can't do anything about this."

"I understand."

APRIL is sitting at the table, working on another one of her playlists. April likes music. She likes the sculptural rhythms of songs when they meld with her brain, and she likes even more how sometimes she can find words in the songs that are important to her. She likes picking all of those songs out and then putting them on playlists when they have a particular theme in common. Then she orders the songs according to some method of which I am not aware. She spends hours making a playlist and, after it is made, she listens to the songs only in that order. Then she syncs her iPod with all these playlists and listens to it when she rides the Metro, so she doesn't have to pay attention to the world around her.

"Are you ready to tell me yet?" she asks, closing her MacBook and getting up from the table. She straddles me on the bed and pins my wrists next to my head. "I'm not going to let you up until you tell me."

"That's just going to make it harder."

"Ah, yes." She moves off me and curls her legs between her arms.

"It's one of the interns. The congressman asked her to come to his apartment and showed up in his bathrobe."

April stands up. "You've been keeping that from me for a whole day?"

"No, listen. I only found out this part today."

"Okay." She sits back down. "Start from the beginning."

I tell her the whole story from being called in on Sunday until my conversation with Rachel today.

"I guess that means there's evidence."

"What do you mean?"

"The jacket. It's still at his apartment, right? I doubt she took it with her when she left."

"Who knows? He probably threw it away. He's not stupid."

"Even smart people make mistakes. Why would he expect anyone else to find it anyway?"

"But that isn't going to be enough to fry this guy. Just a jacket. It doesn't prove what she says happened happened."

"No…But you should at least make her aware of her options. It sounds like she doesn't know she has any."

"Does she?"

"Maybe not, but why should you be the one to decide that for her?"

BETHESDA, doors opening. At the top of the escalator, the same street musician is playing. A crowd of people surrounds him.

Thursday, July 19, 2007

THE congressman is introducing the farm bill to the House along with 20 other co-signers. This is a big day for him. It is his first time introducing legislation—never mind the fact that he wasn't responsible for writing the bill himself. Most of it is earmarks written by lobbyists or, as the congressman likes to call them, "regular folk."

He's talking on the floor when Vicky walks up to my desk. "One of the interns isn't in today."

"What? Who? Did they call in sick?"

"It's Rachel. No, she didn't call. I emailed her and haven't heard anything."

"Rachel. It's not like her not to call."

"You can never tell with these college students. Maybe she's having a mental breakdown or something. What is she? A sophomore?"

"Yeah. Maybe. I don't know." Rachel's emergency contact is her mother. I slide the card back into my drawer.

The congressman doesn't come back to the office that day and, by the evening, he is on his way back to Ohio.

When April asks about Rachel, I tell her she's out sick.

"I hope so."

Friday, July 20, 2007

Rachel doesn't show, but an email shows up in my inbox. "I've had a death in the family. I won't be coming back to work."

"You realize what's happened, don't you?" April is standing by the window and I am at the door. I haven't taken my shoes off. "You did what he asked you to do."

"I didn't do anything."

"Right, you weren't there when she needed it. You missed your chance."

"I'm not sure it's that clear cut."

"How can you say that? That's exactly what happened. You could've given her…something. You chose not to."

"I chose?"

"Yes." April walks away from the window and toward me. "You did."

"What options did I have? To get fired? Quit my job? It wouldn't end with him. I'd be blacklisted. No one would ever hire me again. They always call references in this town. And I can't pretend like I never worked there."

"So what?"

"'So what?'"

"What about the intern? What's she supposed to do now? How's she supposed to get a job? What about her references?"

"I know. I don't know. I don't know."

"I can't believe you were a part of this."

"This goes on all the time. You don't know what it's like."

"What?" April twists her head. "Believe me, I know."

There was a long silence.

"Maybe nothing would happen. But how dare you not try?"

"Is it my place to try?"

"She's a kid. She came to you for help. And you didn't do anything."

Saturday, July 21, 2007

April calls me early in the morning, asking to meet at the park. Dupont Circle, doors opening. Malcolm X Park is a 15-minute walk.

After the concrete walls is the cascading fountain, surrounded by stairs. We meet by the Joan of Arc statue, then start walking.

"It's over, Michael."

"Okay."

"I can't be with someone who doesn't have a moral compass."

She stops by a tree. "I hope you do do something to help that intern. She deserves your try."

She leaves.

I go to sit by the fountain, at the top of the steps.

Monday, July 23, 2007

THE congressman is in the office by eleven, and he notices. He gives me a wide grin.

"You can tell me the story later," he says as he walks toward his office. "I knew I could count on you."

"What was that all about?" Vicky asks.

"The farm bill. Lobbyist stuff."

TRAINS rush to the platform and then stop. Coming as they slow, and they stop. And then go. And go and stop. There at the platform and then gone shooting through the tunnel. Like electrons. Farragut North, doors opening. Rachel walks through the doors.

"Rachel."

She looks in my direction. The train is empty.

"Michael."

"Rachel." I'm standing next to her now.

We both look away.

"Listen, Rachel."

She looks up.

"I hope you aren't leaving for the wrong reasons. That thing you told me about, there are options, you know. You can get a lawyer."

"Why bother? It's not like there's any evidence."

"Didn't you leave anything at his apartment? What about that jacket?"

"I didn't think of that. You think that would be enough?"

"I don't know. Maybe, maybe not. But it's worth a try."

"How? It's not like we can get into his apartment anyway."

"That's not exactly true." I pull my keys out of my pocket and hold one up with my thumb and forefinger. The key has a green ribbon around it. "He'll be out of town Thursday…I can go over on Saturday and take a few photographs." The train fades away, and my bedroom ceiling fades in, still dark. I jut my foot out to knock the sheet off and walk to the bathroom to pee.

Tuesday, July 24, 2007

THE alarm blares. I dial my old English professor before work.

"Professor Boykin."

"Hello, Michael."

"I wanted to talk to you about the intern you sent us. I think she may be mixed up in some trouble and I want to help. Do you have her cell?"

"What kind of trouble? Is everything okay?"

"I just want to check in on her."

"Okay."

"I can't get into it. Maybe I'll tell you when it's all over."

"Sure." He gives me her cell but says one more thing before hanging up: "I hope you're keeping our promise."

CAPITOL South, doors opening.

The phone rings as soon as the clock strikes 9 am. It's Vicky. "There's a reporter with *The Washington Post* on the phone. Jennifer Baker."

"Did she say what it was about?"

"No."

"Transfer me the call."

"This is Jennifer Baker with *The Washington Post*. We're publishing an article on allegations that Congressman Taylor sexually harassed an intern. Does the congressman have any comment before we go to print?" Rachel must have talked to the reporter.

"Sir?"

"The congressman isn't in yet. He'll be in at 10 am. Can you wait until I speak with him?"

"Yes. And to whom am I speaking?"

"This is Michael. Michael Trenton. I'm the congressman's chief of staff."

"Michael, do you have a comment on the sexual harassment allegations?"

"No."

"Was the office an environment where crude or sexual jokes were made on a regular basis?"

"Not to my knowledge."

"What about the two other staff members who left a month ago? Is that turnover connected to the congressman's behavior?"

"Ms. Baker?"

"Yes?"

"Give me an hour. I'll tell the congressman you called."

"Okay." I hang up.

When the congressman walks in, he calls me into his office. Vicky watches me as I close the door behind us.

"So, what about this story you were going to tell me?" the congressman asks, spinning his chair to face me as he puts his legs up on the desk.

"What story?" I don't sit.

"The intern. How'd you finagle it? You had me worried for a moment."

"Oh. Listen. A journalist from *The Washington Post* called this morning. They're going to run a story on sexual harassment allegations against you. They wanted to know if you had any comment."

The congressman moves his legs off the desk. "What did you just say?"

"Do you have any comment? I told the journalist I'd call her back at ten."

"How are we going to spin this one? I guess we can go the old route. Deny, deny, deny. It wouldn't be the first time." He chuckles.

"You're on your own."

"Excuse me?"

"I quit, sir. I'm calling the journalist back, then I'm going home."

"I see. That's very disappointing."

"Yessir."

"Get out of my office."

"Yessir."

On my way back to my desk, Vicky pulls me over. "That reporter's on the phone again. She started asking me a bunch of questions. I told her I had to put her on hold because you were in a meeting."

"Forward the call to me."

"What are you going to say to her?"

I make my way back to my desk. "Mr. Trenton?"

"Yes, this is he."

"This is Jennifer Baker with *The Washington Post*. I'm calling back about allegations that the congressman sexually harassed members of his staff."

"Yes, Ms. Baker."

"Did you have a chance to speak with the congressman?"

"Yes, I did."

"Does the congressman have any comment on the allegations?"

"You'll have to speak to him directly."

"Okay. I'm outside the office, down the hallway. I'll be in in five minutes."

"You're outside the office?"

"Yes."

"And you're coming here?"

"Yes."

"Okay." I hang up and pick up my jacket, then walk out as Vicky stares at me. I stand outside the door, next to the American flag.

Jennifer Baker appears. She's a thin woman, with brown, curly hair and brown eyes. "Ms. Baker?"

"Yes?"

"You'll find the congressman in his office."

"Where are you going?"

"I've just submitted my resignation."

"Do you have any comment on the recent allegations?"

"No."

"Is your resignation a result of the alleged sexual harassment by the congressman?"

"What do you want me to say, Ms. Baker?"

"I want to know if you have a comment before we go to print. Do you?"

"My comment is that I no longer work for the congressman." I walk to the bathroom and open the window. It's hot out and there's nothing to look at but a roof and the other inner walls of the Cannon Office Building. I pull Rachel's number out of my wallet and stare at it. I put it back in my wallet and walk out the door. The hallway outside of the congressman's office is empty. Maybe the congressman is giving the journalist his old frat boy charm.

***

For a long time, nothing happens. I take a job with a nonprofit. April never calls, and I never call Rachel. The congressman loses his office in 2010, two terms after he started. All our work against the guest worker bill and all the other liberal initiatives never made any difference. He still lost. *The Washington Post* doesn't print the story until 2018 when I had figured it would never come back to haunt me. But they weren't the ones to break the story. Rachel penned an op-ed herself on *Vox*. My name's in her editorial and it's just the way April would have told it. I did nothing. Rachel told me and I did nothing. Then she went to a journalist who seemed ready to print the story but backed out at the last minute, saying her editor "killed the story."

But that's not all. Rachel says something that April and I never talked about. She gives a quote by Malcolm X from an interview that I suddenly remembered Professor Boykin showing a clip of in his class: "'A fox acts friendly toward the lamb and usually the fox is the one who ends up with the lamb chop on his plate. The wolf doesn't act friendly and therefore the wolf has more difficulty in getting the lamb chop on his plate.'" That stung—even more so because I knew I couldn't deny its application to me. I don't lose my new job, but when the college holds my class reunion, I don't go because I know I can't look Professor Boykin and the rest of them in the face.

Alexander Etheridge

LIVING WILL

We go on,
the blind lives,
dusting for prints. The center is everywhere,
the atmosphere's smell like a great fire.
We kept a prayer book of paper cuts.
Our walk to the killing floor—a caught breath
of praise.
A fire going out.
Note on our door with a map
leading through trap doors. Hail five thousand years
of cell mates
family plots and pottery dust.
The library of Eden willed to
a blizzard of relapsing fever.
Rubble-glass and hacking cough. Timeline of higher thought
like having bad dreams.
Drawn blank by doctoral candidates—
March all morning through dark

while storms raid the sea.
Hail Wintertide. Relic of whispers,
one word, maybe one
crossing over.

They were so different from the tastefully-covered and carefully-footnoted Penguins I'd read and taught as an academic.

Cathy Shuman

SUCH REST

ON planes and days off I prefer science fiction, but for twenty years, every night before falling asleep, I've been reading the novels of Charlotte M. Yonge. I have favorites I've read dozens of times; there are others I revisit rarely. As I am finishing one I can usually figure out which one I want next.

One of the best-selling authors of the Victorian era, Yonge was born in 1823, published her first novel at 21, and kept writing till her death at 78. Henry James saw "the force of genius" in her breakout hit *The Heir of Redclyffe* (1853). She wrote biography, history, and criticism as well as fiction, virtually invented the young-adult novel for girls, and served as the editor of a monthly magazine for 50 years. These days, though, she is hardly known except among academics, where she's one of those "marginalized women writers" useful for another example of something or other in nineteenth-century British fiction: stepmothers, fossil collecting, mining disasters. A few of her novels were briefly in print in the 1990s when recovering obscure women writers was a thing, but none are in print now.

There's a good reason for that. Yonge's ultraconservative identity politics have not worn well. Her novels are explicitly antifeminist, antidemocratic, and jingoistic, fervently Christian while completely lacking in religious tolerance. A very smart friend of mine, one of the few people I have talked into trying Yonge, wrote to me about reading *Heartsease* (1854):

> I'd gotten about a third of the way through, and was really enjoying it! Of course I despised every single character, and the author, and the social system that had produced them, but in a fun way…But then I got to this bit:

> ...*the practical life in the most trivial round can be united with ... casting all our care upon Him—the being busy in our own station with choosing the good part. I suppose it is as a child may do its own work in a manufactory, not concerning itself for the rest; or a coral-worm make its own cell, not knowing what branches it is helping to form, or what an island it is raising.*

Yes, that passage makes even me wince every time I read *Heartsease*—child labor in a factory depicted as not only acceptable, but potentially sacred, not to mention on a level with a coral-worm building its reef. Where is the outrage over working-class exploitation that we find in more familiar authors, the darkness of Blake's Satanic mills, the preciousness of Dickens's little Nell?

Yonge—the squire's daughter in a small village near Winchester, England—led a quiet life. She read (in seven languages), she wrote (sometimes working on three manuscripts at a time), and assisted the local vicar with the charitable tasks suitable for a gentlewoman. Her vicar—and mentor—was poet and theologian John Keble, the author of the wildly popular *Christian Year* (1827), and one of the leaders of the Anglican Church's Oxford Movement. The "Tractarians" (as they were also called) insisted on an unbroken chain of sanctity reaching from the original Church of Biblical times to the nineteenth-century Church of England, excluding both Roman Catholicism and non-Anglican Protestantism. Being Christian was thus not merely a matter of one's relationship to God. It involved membership in the community of the Anglican Church, most powerfully through participation in its rites. Many Britons distrusted the Tractarian emphasis on Church ritual and power. The movement's most famous leader, John Henry Newman, weakened the group's influence irreparably by converting to Catholicism in 1845, well before Yonge's major novels started appearing in the 1850s. Nevertheless, she remained a staunch Churchwoman and devoted adherent to Tractarian theology.

So why do I find myself narrating 21st-century life to Yonge's ghost when riding the bus? She listens appreciatively to my explanations of cars, social justice, and pants for women, but in my more reasonable moments, I know my attraction would never be reciprocated. I was born into a secular Jewish family in New York City, raised on liberal politics, and joyfully embraced feminist, Marxist, and postcolonial literary theory in graduate school. Theoretically, I'm an atheist (though given the state of physics these days, anything is possible). In practice, I'm under the sway of a form of magical thinking whereby picturing and genuinely dreading the worst can prevent it from happening. The Christian story of incarnation and atonement, complexly and gorgeously resonant as it is, has never struck me as in the least likely. A vulgar Jew, a strong-minded woman, an unbeliever: I could never have fit into any space of the actual woman's imagination except as some kind of monster or joke.

I STARTED reading Yonge for work. In the late 1990s, shortly before being denied tenure at my first academic job, I was working on a book about the novelistic depiction of clergymen leaving the Anglican Church. A fellow-Victorianist mentioned Yonge, so I read *The Heir of Redclyffe* because it's her best-known. I enjoyed the complexity of the characterization, but none of the major characters were clergymen. "Try *Magnum Bonum* [1879] or *The Young Stepmother* [1861]," my friend suggested, but I never really found a good fit for my book. Although Yonge personally knew some of the clergymen who left the Church of England in the wake of Newman's conversion, an Anglican priest giving up his cure is inconceivable in her fictional world. But I kept reading anyway: *The Daisy Chain* (1856), *The Trial* (1864), *Clever Woman of the Family* (1865) ....

I don't remember feeling passionate about those first readings—there was no across-a-crowded-room moment of discovery that Yonge was "the one." But as my tenure case languished in the toils of appeal committees and university politics, I'd come home and curl up on a doubled-over mattress shoved into a corner of my study, devouring one Yonge after another, the university library's hardcovers slipping out of their piles to rub against my arm, my lips sore and salty from binging on sunflower seeds. Cleaning out the apartment when I left, I found bits of their soft gray shells stuck in the crevice between wall and floor. As a perhaps not-very-effective act of revenge, I copied hundreds of pages of those hardcovers on the English Department's Xerox machine (on the university's dime, you see). And if you care for books as well as writing, you'll be scandalized to hear that I enjoyed hearing the bindings crack as I laid each page flat.

Appeal denied, I moved my Xeroxed Yonge from the Midwest to New York City, joining my husband Phil and getting a job at an academic database. My commute included a view of the Statue of Liberty and I relished office gossip and office ritual, but I admit to some intellectual restlessness. I worked intermittently on my book, but mostly I just kept reading and re-reading Yonge. And collecting: those Xeroxes were awkward to read and there's just the right amount of difficulty in finding the books of a prolific but out-of-print author. On trips to visit Phil's family in England, we'd drive to Hay-on-Wye, a whole town (I kid you not) of used book stores, crowned with a ruined castle and set in the midst of almost comically gorgeous scenery on the Welsh border. And although most of her major novels were written for adults, they were also to be found in a tiny shop in Cambridge that sold used children's books. You went up a tight curving staircase and found yourself surrounded by rows of Enid Blyton and E. Nesbit. At the end of the very last row there'd be about six inches of dark-blue Yonges, published by MacMillan and Co., with her initials on the front in fancy gold lettering: CMY.

They were so different from the tastefully-covered and carefully-footnoted Penguins I'd read and taught as an academic. They had a kind of solidity, an objecthood, that kept you aware of their literal origin in Victorian presses, Victorian lending libraries and bookshops. Once or twice I even had to cut open the pages. There's something almost illicit about reading that kind of book in bed—as if I'd smuggled them out of their proper context into our nest of skin and sheets, pillows, cough drops, Kleenex, Phil interrupting with a funny bit from *The New Yorker*. The blue would sometimes come off on my fingers, and the corners of the pages crumbled. Getting back into bed always involved sweeping away triangular shards of creamy-yellow paper scattered in the sheets. Phil would complain, and then make fun of my American pronunciation of *Dynevor Terrace* (1857).

Eventually I'd acquired copies of all Yonge's major novels several times over, and the Internet kind of took the fun out of book collecting. A few years ago I got a Kindle, which now contains (among other things) Yonge's complete novels for $4.99. No more page-cutting, blue fingers, or tiny triangles stuck to my skin. But I still feel that time-traveler's joy in incongruity. Reading Yonge, you can't avoid the thrill of difference, the blending of a totally alien value system with a still-recognizable depiction of everyday life.

ONE of the joys of novel-reading is finding the bland details of actual life (or, even better, actual life in the past) transfigured by transportation into the magical realm of literature. If Yonge is still celebrated for anything, it's her close attention to the minutia of Victorian middle-class life, from servant-hiring to dress shopping to school routine. In *The Pillars of the House* (1873), Geraldine Underwood winces at the "grinding sensation" of unpicking the seams of a dress. Her brother Felix probes another sister's feelings about a new suitor as he "walk[s] up to [her] to fold together the sheets they were stripping" from a bed. For the devout Yonge, the Incarnation—Christ's human embodiment—imbues the most mundane human action with religious significance. Everything about material reality is as well worth our attention as Holy Scripture. "The practical life in the most trivial round," coral worms and working-class children—all are equally important to God. When, in *Dynevor Terrace*, three-year-old Kitty Frost decides that her two-year-old sister ought not to have a paper knife and hits her over the head with it, every move in their "petty squabbles" is both instantly recognizable to any reader who's been around young children, and at the same time imbued with moral (though not moralistic) significance.

It's so easy for us to either universalize or condescend to the Victorians. I could try to argue (in a well-established literary-critical tradition) that Yonge's vivid depiction of her reality means that underneath her reactionary pose, there's a repressed rebel available to the deft and careful reader. Quite honestly, though, there really isn't. Anyway, that kind of reading against the grain is nothing like the comfortingly unironic way I read Yonge's novels every night. But she *could* be said to subvert her time's novelistic (if not political or religious) orthodoxy. Perhaps in part because Yonge herself never married, she tends to eschew the time-honored "marriage plot" culminating in the protagonist's selection of a mate. In *Hopes and Fears* (1860), *The Daisy Chain*, and *Pillars of the House*, for example, central female characters make explicit decisions to live single. And *The Young Stepmother*, *The Three Brides* (1876), *Magnum Bonum*, and *Heartsease* (among others) chronicle their heroines' married lives, not their courtships.

In *Heartsease* we meet the proud, rebellious noblewoman Theodora Martindale and her middle-class sister-in-law, Violet. Theodora is pretty much your conventionally unconventional Victorian heroine, struggling away from self-assertion towards the right marriage at novel's end. But Violet is something else. A timid, simpering, fretful, greeting-card-pretty 16-year-old with psychological superpowers, she is already married to Theodora's frat-boy brother Arthur when we meet her in Chapter Two. Arthur, while good-natured and affectionate, spends the novel hunting, fishing, and ruining the family at the races while the sickly, humble Violet is left to deal with their financial problems and frequently-appearing children. Unlike troublesome spouses in more familiar Victorian fiction (think of *Jane Eyre* or *Middlemarch*), Arthur is still alive and well at novel's end. By then, however, through selflessness, religious faith, and various acts of emotional blackmail, Violet has cured the entire Martindale family of pride, materialism, self-absorption, flirting, gambling, and tuberculosis.

I admit that who-will-she- (or occasionally, he) marry remains a central question in many of Yonge's novels. But even her marriageable young girls aren't always what we expect of nineteenth-century heroines. While even I have trouble with Violet, Phoebe Fulmort of *Hopes and Fears* is one of my favorite Yonge characters. The middle daughter of a wealthy family, she spends most of the novel providing dutifully selfless support to her developmentally challenged, precocious, dissipated, self-righteous, shrewish, or self-indulgent siblings. She's intelligent but no genius, pleasant-looking rather than beautiful or plain. She enjoys shopping and is not above looking forward to a ball, remaining untouched by romantic desire till page five hundred and something, when she falls in love with and quickly marries the heir of the neighboring estate. To 21st-century readers of 19th-century fiction, trained on the brilliant, rebellious, passionate, poor, and/or orphaned heroines of Brontë, Eliot, and Austen, she might sound annoying or tedious. But Phoebe is no priggish nonentity.

Early in *Hopes and Fears*, the handsome but dissolute Owen Sandbrook teases Phoebe, whom he discovers studying political theory in obedience to her strict governess:

> "... There's no act of tyranny a woman in authority will not commit. But this is a free country, Phoebe, as maybe you have gathered from your author, and unless her trammels have reached to your soul –" and he laid his hand on the book to take it away.
>
> "Perhaps they have," said Phoebe, smiling, but holding it fast, "for I should be much more comfortable in doing as I was told."
>
> "Indeed!" said Owen, pretending to scrutinize her as if she were something extraordinary (really as an excuse for a good gaze upon her pure complexion and limpid eyes, so steady, childlike, and unabashed, free from all such consciousness as would make them shrink from the playful look). "... Now, in my experience the comfort would be in *not* doing as you were told."

How can there be a novel heroine who wants only to do as she is told? It's a truism that fictional characters are basically clothed desires. As Owen suggests, fictional plots can only arise out of their desire to have things otherwise than as they are. But Phoebe's happy obedience proves the unexpected source of action as well as strength and generosity.

The epitome of feminine propriety, she is nevertheless more hero than heroine: braving county gossip, thwarting a burglary, and saving siblings' lives several times over. She has no will outside the conventions of familial duty and proper femininity, and yet she emerges as one of the novel's most vivid characters. There's no need for me to read against the grain to find Yonge's work alluringly unconventional. Characters like Violet and Phoebe irradiate and transform our stifling, normative, *Handmaid's Tale* clichés of traditional Victorian culture.

READING, rereading, collecting—the history of fandom suggested an obvious next step in my Yonge fixation. I started planning a pilgrimage to Otterbourne, Yonge's home town. We were in England to attend Phil's stepsister's wedding in a sixteenth-century manor house (beautiful wedding, disastrous marriage). Afterwards, Phil was going to research the arcane world of 20th century art music at the British Library and I would wander around London, feeling nostalgic for the year I'd spent there after college working in a bookshop, pogoing at punk gigs, and exploring life beyond the middle class. But maybe I'd also take a day trip to Winchester, where there was a Cathedral and other touristy things to do and from which I could get a bus that went to Otterbourne, only four miles away. It would be a charmingly idiosyncratic way to flaunt my charmingly idiosyncratic Yonge obsession and act out on a little bit of research envy ("I have an object of study too, babe"). But fate intervened—I caught a nasty flu from the stepsister's groom and ended up shivering and coughing for three days in a borrowed London flat that was freezing cold and empty of everything but an incredibly loud toilet and the third Harry Potter book. Flew 4000 miles for that.

I kept reading Yonge every night, but it took me over ten years to return to the idea of visiting Otterbourne, now referring to it somewhat nervously as "research for this thing I'm writing." By then, Phil and I had moved from New York to North Carolina and I was teaching again, creative nonfiction rather than Victorian novels. A bus still went from Winchester to the White Horse Inn at Otterbourne—indeed had done so at least since Yonge's biographer Georgina Battiscombe got off there in 1941. And while most of Yonge's surviving papers are at Oxford, Winchester's Hampshire Record Office had some letters and clippings—worth checking out, if only for a taste of the archive experience. Phil was going to a conference in London, and we'd visit his parents in Birmingham. A plan emerged.

But as we boarded our flight, I felt faintly embarrassed about the whole thing. Yonge lived with her family in the house she was born in till at age 35 she moved about 100 yards down the High Street where she lived for another 43 years before crossing the road to her current location, the churchyard of St. Matthew's Church. While she set novel episodes in Malta, Peru, and the Pacific Islands, she herself travelled very little. How would she have regarded my expedition? Certainly the Oxford Movement wasn't *against* pilgrimages, and several of them visited the Holy Land. Yonge's generation had a tendency to romanticize the Crusades and she donated the proceeds of *The Heir of Redclyffe* to fund a missionary ship. But, as she's always ready to remind her readers, home responsibilities and duties come first. Every time you entered an Anglican church you were on a pilgrimage, connecting with the sacred. Anyway, the Holy Land would doubtless be full of untrustworthy foreigners.

So what exactly was I after? I could find photographs of Otterbourne, then and now, on the Internet, and Yonge's letters, thoroughly footnoted and contextualized, through the Charlotte M. Yonge Fellowship website. Even as an academic writer I'd never been into biographies or archives—was this pilgrimage going to tell me anything about Yonge I couldn't find on Pinterest? Given this already-problematic analogy between religious faith and a perverse crush on an obscure author, wasn't I already as close to Yonge's world as I needed to be?

George Eliot and Karl Marx, two of my more canonical Victorian crushes, are buried around the corner from each other in Highgate Cemetery, so before I left London for Winchester I visited it as a kind of trial run. Its beauty surprised me. Deep woods gathered about 100 yards from the entrance, like a spooky setting for a supernatural tale. I walked down long gloomy aisles, with tall trees almost meeting overhead, dark and pale green against the gray sky. The ground rose on either side, crowded with gravestones, ghostly white, mushroom-gray, marked out with splashes of purple and red flowers, or choked with weeds and disintegrating in attractive ways.

Marx has two graves, actually. In 1954, he and several family members were dug up from their initial inconspicuous spot, moved to a more central location, and marked by a towering plinth topped by a mammoth head with a jutting beard and dark pits for eyes. Cartoon Marx. I was surprised to see quite a crowd leaning against the graves across the way, snapping photos. His original grave is deep in the woods, a flat stone you can hardly read his name on. But it had been visited too, as you could tell from the little arrangements of stones spaced evenly around the edges, a few red candles in jars, and a bunch of red plastic flowers. I only saw one other person there, a young woman who seemed a bit startled when I asked if she knew the meaning of the stones. She guessed that they were Tibetan or Indian. Later I remembered that's a Jewish custom, putting pebbles on graves.

Eliot's marker was less impressive—a plain granite pillar overlooking a bed of weeds and rising out of a closely-packed row on a hill off the main walkway. There were pebbles there too, but (as I saw with delight) mostly there were pens. Ordinary ballpoints, felt tips, roller balls—some with slips of paper tucked in their clips, which I wished I dared take out to read. They were stuck in close together like a crop coming up, almost buried in clover. It felt like I ought to have known about this custom, but when I Googled it later all I found was one Instagram mention, not even a picture. I rummaged in my bag for a Pilot Precise V5 Extra Fine, and stuck it in towards the back.

At Highgate, I didn't think about Eliot or Marx actually being there (their bodies or skeletons or spirits or whatever). There's probably not an inch of ground—at any rate in well-settled countries like England or the U.S.—that doesn't have human remains mixed in it somehow. Dead people themselves aren't more in one place than anywhere else. But the pens, the pebbles, Marx's big head, the bright flowers against the gray stone—they marked a true connection between the living and the dead: a beautiful thing.

A few days later, Yonge's grave in Otterbourne Churchyard looked surprisingly modern. It was in a stone like Eliot's, but horizontal, like Marx's original: a cross in a frame on the ground with the inscription running round the outside. I found a place where the weeds had eaten into the stone so I could stick a pen into the dirt, with a bit of paper under the clip saying "to CMY from CS." It really oughtn't to have been different from Highgate, but the shiny plastic and raw white paper looked incongruous rather than touching in that gentle, ancient place. The pen in the grave is an easy gesture—an offline "like"—but speaking *as* a writer *to* a writer is no simple thing. I wonder sometimes if it got removed later as desecration. I hope not.

ONE of the Oxford Movement's central tenets was the "Doctrine of Reserve," the idea of the essential privacy, even secrecy, of religious feeling. Unlike Evangelicals or "Low Church" Anglicans, Tractarians did not believe that Christians should declare their faith in personal testimony. Rather, they should *enact* it quietly and unobtrusively, leading a virtuous life, obeying the Ten Commandments, and participating in Church ritual. As the Revd. Isaac Williams puts it in "On Reserve in Communicating Religious Knowledge," the good Christian's life is "a self-denying and consistent performance of religious duties in secret." We should emulate Christ, who longs to share salvation with humanity, but nevertheless only shows it indirectly, through the parables and actions we find in Scripture. Like "genuine poetry," religious truth is not something that can be summarized, defined, or grasped immediately. It must be felt, absorbed, interpreted. Like the Gospels themselves, good Christians must show, not tell; our creative writing cliché was their central moral precept. By making no professions, simply acting selflessly, characters like Violet and Phoebe instruct their families and acquaintances as well as their readers. At a family crisis, for example, Phoebe shows her restless brother Mervyn how to wait:

> Only that which has substance can be motionless. There she sat in the lamplight, her head drooping, her hands clasped on her knee, her eyes bent down, not drowsy, not abstracted, not rigid, but peaceful. Her brother lay in the shade, watching her with a half-fascinated gaze, as though a magnetic spell repressed all inclination to work himself into agitation.

The Oxford Movement's doctrine enables Yonge to create characters like Violet and Phoebe, outwardly conformist, inwardly—not, indeed, rebellious, but more deeply, secretly faithful. Perhaps her biographer Battiscombe suggests the key to understanding the "peculiar effect" of reading Yonge: she "make[s] ordinary, everyday goodness appear the most exciting thing in the world."

Winchester looks like any English country town. The streets curl gently, like sideways rolling hills, lined with terraces of improbably tiny white stucco or red brick houses, with doors right up on the narrow sidewalk. Coming back from the supermarket to my Airbnb on the first night, I walked behind a woman with two raincoated children, teasing each other. Suddenly she stopped right in front of me and unlocked a door, whisked the children in and closed it firmly behind her. An Alice in Wonderland moment.

At the Hampshire Record Office the next day, I opened a gray cardboard folder tied in white ribbon, surprised to find myself tearing up and trembling at the sight of Yonge's handwriting. I laughed and excused myself to the tall, kindly young man with a thick provincial accent who'd handed me the file—"ah, you have to take a minute, do you?" he teased gently.

> My dear Miss Bourne:
>
> Our difficulties are so far lefsened that the married servant I mentioned once to you can come for a few months to teach both house and kitchen work, so I do not think I shall take a laundrefs unless some very splendid ready made article

should turn up, as we do not want to have too many people about, and hope to keep Mrs. Attwood till after June for the sake of her experience and sick cookery.

Good, clear handwriting filled up every inch of blue and rustling sheets like airmail paper, but of course it wasn't airmail. One or two letters were "black-bordered," a mourning thing I'd read about in novels but never actually seen. I also hadn't realized that you can tell how long a nibful of ink lasts (about ten lines) before it starts to fade; she writes till the last word is almost illegible. The ts are crossed with hair-thin dashes, and she still uses the long form "s" when the letter is doubled. It did make me hungry for more than that random glimpse, but I also got a kick out of its very randomness, the specificity and immediacy of those nine letters lying so close to where she had written them. No thickly-stuffed folder handed me by some bored silent page in a high-ceilinged, oak-paneled Oxford library would have that.

As I returned the folder to the friendly clerk, he must have been Googling Yonge, because he looked up from his screen to tell me about a statue of her sitting on a bench at Eastleigh train station, one stop from Winchester. So the next day, when the Record Office closed at 5:00, I boarded a train jammed full of commuters from London. Yonge never lived in Eastleigh, but when she donated £500 in 1868 to build a parish church, she was asked which of its two villages the parish should be named after, Barton or Eastley. She chose Eastley, but asked that it be spelled "Eastleigh," which she saw as "more modern." So she could be called, as she is in the article in the *Southern Daily Echo* where I learned all this, "the Godmother of Eastleigh."

No town is at its most picturesque right outside its train station, but despite its being ranked "9th best place to live in the UK" in 2006, I got the impression that Eastleigh was a dump. "Industrial" was the term the Record Office clerk had used. Its most famous former inhabitant is Benny Hill. The station was definitely not in the classic Victorian Cathedral style, more the midcentury shed style. And it was raining. But there she was, life-sized, in bronze resin, sitting reading on a bench not 100 yards away with her back to the entrance, as promised and pictured online. Next to her a plaque is nailed to the bench:

> Charlotte Mary Yonge (1823-1901)
> Local author and teacher who gave Eastleigh its name.
> Created by Vivien Mallock in 2015.

For some reason I pictured Vivien Mallock as a local near-amateur, with wisps of dark hair escaping from a messy bun, her many-colored scarves fluttering as she talked earnestly and non-stop to convince the town council to make this bizarre decorating choice on vaguely feminist grounds. I could not have been more wrong. Mallock has a national reputation and the statue is part of a carefully-planned series of public artworks in the area, designed to call attention to Eastleigh's "cultural heritage." It's supposed to depict Yonge at 45, her age when she gave the money for the church, but it fits a huge, aged, harsh-featured face onto a young, slim body, so it seems both insultingly literal and too generic. There's a book lying in her lap, which I wasted considerable time trying to decipher, but it's only an artist's impression of text, not real words at all. Later, I learned that, though since repaired, the statue's nose had been chipped off by vandals before it was officially unveiled. "Not a real surprise—there aren't too many literary fans in Eastleigh," commented "Mr. Southampton" on the news reported online in the *Southern Daily Echo*.

I spent about 10 minutes taking pictures in the rain, trying for a decent selfie, but both of us looked hideous. No doubt I afforded entertainment to the guy sitting smoking in front of the station, talking to his mate across the entrance. I couldn't hear what they were saying, but they were laughing, and I could pretend they were laughing at me. After Eastleigh, when I asked Winchester locals if they'd heard of Yonge, and they said no, I asked if they'd been to the train station and seen the statue. Usually they had. "Oh, that's her?" they'd respond—not, frankly, all that impressed. Yonge was morbidly shy, and her father, Battiscombe tells us, disapproved of her being "'alone in a railway station.'" How she would have hated being out there, on display, in public, in the ugliest and most utilitarian spot of that ugly and utilitarian town, an overfamiliar detail in the working class's commute. But that's the very thing I love about it—there she is, just there (as she is on my Kindle), under a half-grown tree and next to a trash bin, where everyone sees her even if they don't. Reserve in plain sight.

OTTERBOURNE is a few blocks worth of fairly nice houses along the two-lane highway between Winchester and Southampton, including Yonge's birthplace, Otterbourne House (now a block of flats), and her later home, Elderfield House (now a halfway house for ex-convicts). The buses go through every 15 minutes. After visiting Elderfield House, the church (with a lovely angel ceiling), and churchyard, I stopped for lunch at the White Horse, where the waitress directed me towards a somewhat sad constellation of Yonge-related pictures in a corner. Glumly regarding these, I was reminded of my doubts about this trip. There'd been no unexpected revelations, no numinous encounters. My feet hurt and I felt bloated and untidy, incongruous among the brisk, compact natives in their well-fitting clothes.

The pictures of Otterbourne House I'd seen online showed it guarded by iron gates and a serious-looking hedge: very private property. But when I got there I saw a small opening in the hedge, so what the hell, I thought. Once through, I found a parking lot and a poster for a "Cream Tea for Cancer" being held around the back. Though Yonge disapproved of the frivolity and materialism associated with charity bazaars, they serve as important turning points in several of her novels. And here was a genuine garden fete in full cry, with cream teas set out on one table and prizes for the tombola on another, all under a marquee with little pink flags. I mentioned Yonge to a friendly blonde woman named Claire, who said "oh yes, the author—she lived here." She offered me tea and even showed me her flat, with a beautiful round room, all windows. Maybe Yonge wrote there, but I know nothing about Victorian domestic architecture—it could have been added in the 1980s. "Really," she said, "you should meet Guy."

Guy, a tall, skinny man with a kind face, told me that the house had been built in the second half of the 18th century and turned into flats in the 1970s. He showed me his copy of *The Heir of Redclyffe*, one of those blue-and-gold MacMillans. Of course! He shared his first name with Sir Guy Morville, the hero of Yonge's most famous work. He confessed that he hadn't read it, and asked me if he should. I was as hesitant as I always am when people ask me about reading Yonge. "Oh dear," he smiled, "does my namesake come to a sticky end?" (In fact he dies of malarial fever on his honeymoon.) But Guy's link with Yonge went deeper. He'd written a novel himself, featuring an accidental superhero investigating the theft of Winchester's cultural artifacts. As I stood in his bright, empty sitting room (maybe the fireplace was original?) he brought me a copy of *Culture Man: An Adventure*, which he signed at my request. We chatted about the difference between writing his novel and the technical manuals he wrote for his work in telecom, but it was hard for me to concentrate. I couldn't stop thinking how wonderful it was—Claire and Guy and his book and the Cream Tea for Cancer—how strange and wonderful. Before I left he and Claire posed drinking tea and eating strawberries, as I took one more "picture of the natives" and we all laughed.

Yonge's more famous sister-novelist Jane Austen also lived near Winchester. During my visit I kept noting examples of Austen tourism so I could roll my eyes at them. The docent at the Cathedral could recite all kinds of details about the multiple Austen monuments, but hadn't even heard of the reredos constructed in Yonge's memory! (Phil eventually found it for me, once we figured out what a reredos was.) But of course this just proved how much cooler I was than the Janian hordes. When I got home, as I returned to each Yonge novel I felt its scenes shifting and resettling among Winchester's steep streets and the old stone houses near the grand Cathedral, the landscape around Otterbourne of rolling hills, richly green in summer rain, the little church amid its field of gravestones. Half-sentimental, half-smug, I knew that I alone was capable of the aesthetic, emotional, and historical awareness that appreciating her novels required.

"Pride" connotes good things in contemporary culture—parades, rainbows, social justice. Not for us is pride, as it was originally, the most deadly of the Seven Deadly Sins. For Yonge, it was the most damning sin of which her genteel young characters were capable. Her best-known example made *The Heir of Redclyffe* her greatest success: the poor, morally-upright, self-sacrificing Philip Morville self-righteously and unforgivably persecutes his wealthy, titled, yet self-doubting cousin—Guy's unfortunate namesake—who catches his fatal illness while nursing Philip. Philip is redeemed, though—once he survives the fever, inherits Guy's estate, and spends the final hundred pages of the novel in bitter self-loathing, getting shovelful after shovelful of burning coals of shame heaped upon his head. If obedience rather than desire marks the promising Yonge character, losing—not finding—oneself in selfless service (like Guy) or deep humiliation (like Philip) is the goal of every true hero and heroine of her fiction.

When Yonge's *female* characters lose themselves in selflessness, it can look a lot like orthodox Victorian femininity. Even her contemporaries thought it excessive that the *Daisy Chain*'s Ethel May must sacrifice not only scholarly ambition and romance, but even spectacles for her nearsightedness. In *The Clever Woman of the Family*, Rachel Curtis can only be cured of feminism by falling prey to a conman, suffering the scorn of her entire community, indirectly causing a poor child's death, and almost dying herself before marrying a man she'd originally despised. In *Heartsease*, Theodora, rejected by her fiancé and doomed (or so she thinks) to a dull life waiting on her cold family, is told that "safety and peace [are] to be attained by bowing to the dust, to creep beneath a gateway, the entrance to the glorious place"—like Carroll's Alice making herself small to get into the Red Queen's garden. Bowing to the dust is, after all, not only a feminine but a Christian duty, and in Yonge it involves the same loving intimacy that attends the manufacturing child and the coral worm. Yonge's characters—male and female—are always crushed for their own good—in fact, they enjoy it.

But not in some kind of masochistic frenzy, writhing ecstatically under the lash of God's chastening. That would imply a self-dramatizing excess that no self-respecting Tractarian would dream of. In *Heartsease*, Theodora gets a thrill out of the wringing of her "woman's heart," but later realizes that that thrill was really "temper and jealousy." True self-sacrifice—like Violet's or Phoebe's—must be carefully hidden within the confines of convention. So while suffering is certainly glorified in Yonge's Christian world, it is never dramatic, never thrilling. It's instead the coziness, the comfort, the release from responsibility provided by humiliation and selfless suffering that Yonge's characters love.

Like many Victorians, Yonge is fond of depicting sickbeds: in *Heartsease*, Violet suffers a near-fatal illness "that has been almost all happiness," and after being severely burned in a fire, Theodora comments that "it's a good speculation to be ill." Pain in Yonge may not be passionate, but it is nevertheless just as firmly associated with erotic joy as whips and chains in other kinds of literature. Throughout the novels, sickness and sorrow trigger conjugal love. Not only does Alan Ernescliffe court the badly-injured Margaret May in *The Daisy Chain*, in *The Trial* Margaret's brother Tom expects his consumptive bride to be dead within months (though she unexpectedly survives). *Pillars of the House* features a wedding with a bed-bound groom barely recovering from a life-threatening scald and *Clever Woman*'s Rachel spends her honeymoon convalescing from diphtheria. In Yonge's novels, couples like these frequently describe their happiness as "such rest." Every night as I drift off to sleep, they join factory child and coral worm, "casting their cares" on Him with the ease, recklessness, and intimacy that phrase implies.

Another word Yonge's characters use to describe this state of humbled, chastened bliss is "comfort." Like "pride," "comfort" resonates differently for us than it did in Yonge's time. For us, it's the unthinkingly privileged who live in comfort. To be comfortable is to take the easy way out, to be dangerously complacent—even complicit. In an era famous for its upholstery, however, it's perhaps not surprising that the Victorians used "comfort" as the ultimate praise for domestic virtues both physical and spiritual. Mary Ponsonby, "sitting down on the well-stuffed arm-chair" prepared by the aptly-named Miss Faithfulls for their tenants in *Dynevor*

Terrace, pronounces "that people who would not come there did not understand what comfort was." The frequent communicant Yonge would have been very aware that in the 1662 version of the Book of Common Prayer, the Eucharistic officiant invites his congregation to "the most comfortable Sacrament of the Body and Blood of Christ." When Phoebe feels "more comfortable in doing as I was told" or *Pillars*'s Charlie Audley declares his love to Stella Underwood by asking if "you'll let me try to comfort you" in her grief for her drowned twin, domestic bliss and humbled selflessness become one.

Entranced as I am by Yonge's theology of suffering comfort, I must confess that it doesn't have the slightest effect on my actual behavior. In fact, I strive to avoid painful illness and gut-wrenching humiliation, though every now and then I think about giving the joy of obedience and selflessness a try. Reminding myself of my God-apportioned duties as teacher, daughter, or wife, I decide, should surely help me grade another paper, call my father more, or listen sympathetically to Phil droning on about music theory. It never does. I am just as selfish, lazy, and wayward as ever, perhaps more as I get older. It's not, after all, as if I *identify* with Phoebe or Violet—or any of Yonge's characters. And though it seems to be a requirement for enthusiastic girl readers of 19th-century fiction, I never identified with Austen's Elizabeth, Brontë's Jane, or Eliot's Dorothea either. Despite the frequency with which my students use it, I still cringe when I hear the word "relatable"—and not just because the first time was in reference to Sarah Palin. Why open a book only to look into a mirror? In her wonderful essay, "Amongst People," the novelist Yiyun Li confesses that "To read oneself into another person's tale is the opposite of how and why I read. To read is to be with people who, unlike those around one, do not notice one's existence." I can't read Yonge as a Christian, but I can read her with Li's ghostlike selflessness, shedding the intolerable burden of self-consciousness. I can read her with a kind of obedience, refusing to ironize or patronize, accepting her premises and inhabiting her world. This is most certainly not what Yonge had in mind—but I still want to think of my pleasure in her work as a kind of reverence.

SHORTLY after I started reading Yonge, Phil and I went to a family wedding in Oregon and spent a few days at the coast afterwards. There was this crazy hotel right on the ocean, with themed rooms—I think my brother and his wife had Elvis, and we had Shakespeare—or maybe Virginia Woolf? At any rate, after a walk on the beach in the mist, Phil and I lay on an enormous bed with a wine-colored coverlet, surrounded by elaborate furniture. He had a fat new paperback on the space program, with which—despite his fear of flying—he is fascinated. I was starting *Pillars of the House* for the first time, opening the creaky blue covers of Volume One and counting with delight and awe the *thirteen* Underwood siblings whose varied lives and talents the novel was about to chronicle. At our feet, the Pacific ocean rolled between the bedposts.

The ocean is so completely wild, vast, other—and yet you can walk right up to it, get your feet wet. In *The Trial*, Ethel May arrives at the seaside to nurse her convalescent brother and his idealistic friend: "At the edge of the water she stood—as all others stand there—watching the heaving from far away come nearer, nearer, curl over in its pride of green glassy beauty, fall into foam, and draw back." When I lose myself in Yonge's writing, I am back in that room, at that moment, embraced by that wonder and safety—the *comfort* of that bed and that ocean.

BIBLIOGRAPHICAL NOTE: Although the ideas and opinions expressed in this essay—and certainly any errors or misrepresentations—are my own, I was also helped by the information and expertise provided by a range of sources. The most significant of these were *The Charlotte M. Yonge Fellowship Website* (http://www.cmyf.org.uk), *The Letters of Charlotte Mary Yonge*, edited by Charlotte Mitchell, Ellen Jordan, and Helen Schinske (https://discovery.ucl.ac.uk/id/eprint/13734/), Raymond Chapman's *Firmly I Believe: An Oxford Movement Reader* (Canterbury Press, 2006), the brilliant chapter on *The Heir of Redclyffe* in Susan E. Colón's *Victorian Parables* (Continuum, 2012), Georgina Battiscombe's *Charlotte Mary Yonge: The Story of an Uneventful*

Life (Constable, 1943), Gavin Budge's *Charlotte M. Yonge: Religion, Feminism and Realism in the Victorian Novel* (Peter Lang, 2007), and two books by Talia Schaffer: *Novel Craft: Victorian Domestic Handicraft and Nineteenth-Century Fiction* (Oxford University Press, 2011) and *Romance's Rival: Familiar Marriage in Victorian Fiction* (Oxford University Press, 2016).

THIS AFTERNOON'S SACRAMENT

Lizzy desires fruit and you hers.
Her breath on your neck.
Ancient creatures crawl up buildings.
Something sweet in the neighbor's trash.
How many strolled this street, broke into a run,
their reflections left to the puddles?
In the courtyard of Our Lady of Pompeii
ceniza thumbed across foreheads.
La Virgen, photos of the deceased, pooled wax.
                    A ciborium of stones,
tongueless cavern of gray teeth chewing prayers.
              Do you have one?
Behind, yarrow and pigweed break open the city.
A chain-link fence splits it.
      A fig tree.
Your aunt brings her grandson here,
smiles at the men speaking a language she doesn't understand.
Decades ago, flirtation. Stories stretched for days.
Now collared shirts taut over deflated paunches.
                        Medication regimens.
Two dark teardrops, ripe and heavy, refuse to fall.
A foot gingerly lifted, slacks for mass rising above argyle sock.
You worry you will embarrass him but it is you who blushes.
He worked 10 hour shifts 6 days in a row for decades,
fed more children on meager wages than you've spoken to in months.

Or this is what you imagine as he steps aside, says *Gracias, mi hijo.*
You're a boy again, Gringo. Bring an ancestor down his prize.
                Branches shake. Will they break?
No te caigas. Twist, he directs, and you do, twice,
drop the meat into his hands, withered as dried apple.
You have no great ache to be a father but still
you need someone closer to dying to say *yes, you do. you will, you fool,*
to explain how the tree is trimmed and grows back fuller,
how each year's yield falls and rots beneath if
the young who refuse to kneel here don't know how to eat it
                or even if it is eaten.
The grandfather tears it like fresh mango,
like bread, like the flesh of Christ himself,
offers a piece to you and Lizzy.
                God, the mess of it.
Quivering pink larvae, half-digested wasp bits,
viscera of the sacrificed inside an altar.
Vaginal portal to our alien future.
                Shove it in your mouth.
Anticipate transformation and it is bland.
Lizzy thinks the soil of Brooklyn not so nutrient-rich.
Indeed the broken sea anemone, the glistening organ extracted
tastes like parking lot, like city water, pinch of sugar.
You return to the laundromat, dryers hypnotizing patrons,
wrap hot towels around each other, kiss.

Yvonne Higgins Leach

THE ANCIENTS

I refuse to read the plaque at the trailhead
on the disappearance of big-treed forests.
Refuse to read of industrial scale,
mechanized clear-cutting to feed a ravenous
global market. How only ten percent
of the forests of giants remain. How what
was lush, thick and dense is now stagnant air.

Instead, I choose to walk among them
and ponder:

How it goes with the ancients,
fringed with lichen, their bark
flakes and sheds—a look gained
from great age. They soar up
through the centuries, canopies
in tiers of decades gone by. Where ancients
have fallen, sunlight pours down in gaps
and young ones surge skyward.

Below, the soil is dark like ink,
rich like chocolate. Fungi is alive
in the dank underbelly of logs and nooks
and crooks, in the gothic-shaded network
of roots, snags, branches and ferns.

So much becomes nests for birds and dens for bears.
Weathermakers, food creators, holders of
molds and slimes and moss. What is most amazing
I don't know—how what takes centuries to grow
takes longer to die, yet still nurtures life.

"Everybody I know wants to build a pizza oven"
Harry said, "and then they use it once and burn
the pizza and never touch it again."

RELEASE

There was trouble at the school. I could tell even before I got to Richard's classroom. The halls did not carry the warmed-over, cafeteria scent of frozen potatoes and canned meat, or the sweet, clear smell of elementary-age sweat. It was not antiseptic, soapy. There was no hint of wood-chips or hamster, dried-out basketballs and wrestling mats. It tugged on no memory of mine. It reminded me of nothing.

I waited outside the door of Mr. Byrie's third-grade classroom, my click-clacking laminated visitor pass barely secured to my polo. I could see Richard through the glass window of the door, his hand raised so high his red wooly coat was beginning to slip off his shoulders. It seemed like an inappropriate time to walk in and extract him, so I stayed put, saw Mr. Byrie call on him, tried to make out what Richard was saying, understood it was *bathroom*, saw Mr. Byrie roll his eyes and point to the Smart Board where times tables were written out in the jagged, shaky hand of a Parkinson's patient, saw Richard stand up anyway, heard Mr. Byrie through the glass say, "No, sit back down," and I pushed open the door and looked right at Mr. Byrie.

"I'm picking up my son Richard," I said, trying not to let my lisp melt away the edges of my words. "He has a doctor's appointment. And just so you know, we are not paying 15,000 dollars for you to tell him when he can and cannot go to the bathroom."

Richard stood up too fast and tried to pack up his things in a hurry.

"Mr. Tevis, hello," Mr. Byrie said, "I'm very very sorry—"

"They're third graders," I said, trying to think what somebody stern and authoritative would say. "I really can't believe this. Richard, come on. I'm going to be telling the principal. Or superintendent. Or—whoever you answer to."

"Mr. Tevis, again, my apologies—"

"You do not get to police my son like that. *Richard.*"

He finally came, and I held the door open for him, seething. Mr. Byrie had a sick look on his face but kept his mouth closed.

I led Richard back down the halls, feeling a hard pounding in my chest. The school suddenly filled with the smell of blood and onions and the bitter tang of cocaine. I let myself feel strong and righteous. I straightened out my neck like some emu that had just saved his son from a dingo.

"Here," I said, stopping outside the bathroom. "Mr. Byrie can go to hell."

"It's okay, Chris," Richard said. He pulled his backpack straps tighter around his body. "I don't really have to go anymore."

I WAITED for Richard to bring up the incident at dinner that night. We were having caramelized Brussels sprouts and salmon slick with a dark ginger glaze, like it had just been plucked from an oil spill.

"Check-up went okay?" Harry asked as he cut up a singular Brussels sprout, letting the layers fall away one by one.

"Nothing haywire," I said.

"Only allergies," Richard said.

"Means you have a good immune system," Harry said. "What's going on at school? Are you still in this godawful geologic unit?"

I looked to Richard, gave an easy nod, to reassure him that I was here, would back him up once he told the story.

"I like the rocks," he said. He ate his Brussels sprouts like he was some vegan zealot, not a third-grade boy. "I think fossils are cool. It's like x-rays of the past."

"Very astute," Harry said.

I waited for Richard to continue, say something more, but he was too focused on his dinner.

"Do you know Mr. Byrie well?" I said to Harry.

He shrugged, began peeling another Brussels sprout. "Not outside conferences."

"Mr. Byrie wouldn't let Richard use the bathroom today."

"Was it during an important lesson?"

Richard nodded. "I mean, multiplication—"

"Harry," I said. "What are we going to do? We need to call the school. Get him replaced. It's sadistic."

"Richard? Are you traumatized?"

"No," he said.

"Don't lead him into an answer like that," I said.

"Like what?"

"You can't tell a child that they can't use the bathroom—"

"I'm not a *child*," Richard said.

"It's a classroom," Harry said. "Sometimes you have to wait."

"You're so old. They could slap you with rulers when you were in school. Things are different now."

"I'm not that old, my god."

"I can't believe you're not outraged at this."

"May I be excused?" Richard said.

"No," I said, before realizing it weakened my position. "Well. If you want to you can."

"Go," Harry said to Richard, then looked at me. "Are you okay?"

"What do you mean, am I okay? I'm upset. For Richard."

Harry chewed up the remainder of his Brussels sprout, unsticking a piece from his teeth. "Chris," he said, "maybe it would help if you started running again."

BEFORE I met Harry, when I was still in LA, I ran five days a week, even when I was hungover or coked out from the night before. That had ended after Harry and I got together. Habits are the easiest thing in the world to break when you're with someone new. Especially someone like Harry.

I pulled out the Nikes that my mom had gotten me a couple Christmases ago, hoped they could withstand my heavy, club-footed stride. Richard was at school, Harry at work, and the maid wasn't coming until the afternoon, so I had the place to myself. I spent twenty minutes looking at myself in athletic gear in the bathroom mirror, trying to remember when I had turned so ugly, then reminded myself that nobody's appearance was real, the only thing that existed was tangled optic nerves, the only thing that mattered was the river stone in my belly that diverted the waters of fear and worry and insecurity pouring through me into gentler, shallower pools of peace.

I felt very calm. I said out loud, "You are not ugly." I left Harry's house and started to run.

Two years into marriage, I still felt like a visitor moving through the neighborhood, or some psycho obsessed with peering into windows and seeing all the nice things that you could get when you had money. It was hard not to stare, even now. Every house was like some furniture showroom. There were high golden chairs with coiled wooden legs, paintings from worldwide exhibitions, clean, white, open spaces that felt like the strange video games I saw in my dreams, and gates, gates everywhere.

I was halfway to the bottom of the hill when I felt a slow-trickling itch move up my thigh. I tried not to attack my legs with my fingernails, even as I shuddered and clenched my teeth as I felt the licks of poison under my skin, had to give in and scraped and scraped until there were deep grooves in my flesh. The rash exploded, bloomed, became something even stronger and more tortuous, and I nearly screamed out for some maintenance guy tending one of the million dollar lawns to come over and hack off my legs.

"Richard," I said at 8:30. "I'll tuck you in."

He looked at me, clean and showered and smelling like peach shampoo, and turned away.

"Fine," he said. He went up the stairs. I followed. In his office, I heard Harry on the phone.

Richard's room was filled with compendiums of old 50s comics and pictures of waterfalls and jungle vistas. It alway made me sad to be in his room, and to feel the sick understanding that Richard was not, and would never be, cool.

"Okay," I said as he crawled into bed. "Good night. I love you."

Richard nodded. "Good night."

I turned off the light but lingered by the switch.

"You know," I said, "I will always be there for you. I will always fight for you."

Richard was silent except for his sweet breathing. Finally he made some small noise.

"Thanks," he said.

In the living room, I reminded myself that feelings were only strange, electric discharges. They were prone to change. One day, Richard's brain would spark in the right part of his cortex to make him understand how much his dad fought for him. He would think of me of his dad then, and be overcome by a sudden rush of gratefulness. Or guilt. I was okay with either.

THE hardest part of living a perfect life was filling the days. All my old friends were still at their barista jobs far away in LA, all of Harry's friends were executives on Tokyo time, and so far nobody would let me into the Chapel Hill Support Group for Breastfeeding Moms. It felt exclusionary. Sometimes I went on internet mommy forums to find helpful tips and practice correct swaddling techniques to hypothetically impress them, even though Richard was eight now and I hadn't even known him when he was a baby.

I wondered if my sperm was as strong and hale as Harry's, if it could take to a womb, if it could ever produce a baby that I could hold. I doubted it. Every time I went through TSA screening machines I felt something ferromagnetic happen inside my dick that made me suspect the x-rays had made me sterile.

The only other person I knew who was living a perfect life was Nina. She had been Harry's surrogate, carried Richard for those nine months and three weeks, and handed him over with a smile and a businessman's handshake. We were each other's weekday coffee dates. Harry had set up a healthy fund for Nina and continued to mostly finance her life, so we had a lot in common. She was trying to kickstart her own side-hustle, as she called it, but was always vague on details. I was on some email list she'd made, and sometimes received strange dispatches around 3 AM filled with broken chains of letters and corrupted GIF sets. She said she was still working out the kinks.

One other group of housewives was in our coffee shop, next to a slim little blonde guy with half-stubble and a faggy face. I wondered if he knew where the good gay bars in town were.

"That is totally fucked," Nina was saying, unwrapping an improperly baked croissant. "The whole bathroom shaming thing just makes sweet, beautiful kids like Richard develop a completely fucked relationship with their body and their needs."

"Completely," I said. "And Richard won't even thank me for standing up for him."

"That's probably my family's stubbornness," she said. "The last thing anybody in my family wants is to give anybody else some satisfaction. It's repressed Protestantism or something."

"Did you go to private school, Nina?"

"The closest private school was some academy fifty miles away that's grooming grounds for military intelligence. Fuck no. I barely went to public school."

"Exactly, same as me. These private schools—I don't know. They're weird. Like it's some big drafty house that's being staged for a real estate showing. Every sign of life feels fake."

"Maybe you should talk to Harry about moving Richard to a different school."

I drank some of my berry tea, knew immediately that would be a losing battle.

"Probably won't do that," I said. "He knows what he wants for Richard."

"Do you know what you want for him?"

"I think my opinion is less valuable."

"Well," Nina said. "You can suffer in silence, then."

I'M down in West Hollywood and somehow got there by bus. By *bus*. The friends I'm with are drunk and high out of their mind, poppers have been shared, and we don't know anybody but somehow manage to cut the line for the club and no one's mad at us.

Nobody I'm with has coke, so I root around for it like a truffle-hunting pig, sniffing in the least discreet way possible, going up to the sketchiest-looking strangers first and making sad lamb-y eyes at them. I am not thinking about children's size six shoes, or allergy medication, or why the worksheets they make third-graders do are so complicated and strange. I am thinking: *fuck this music is shitty, why won't they just play fucking Madonna, shit I really look like this, holy fuck why does my throat taste like an auto-repair shop.*

I get coke, I always get coke, and then I don't think about a lot. I make out with a stranger whose face keeps changing under the lights, and I'm not sure if it's my fault or his. I'm not thinking about anything when I start crying, for some reason this coke is making me do that, and I cry harder because I miss the days they just cut it with caffeine, not whatever fiendish, mind-altering irritant that's causing this weeping. Meth, probably. All my friends are gone, doing something illicit in the bathroom or following strangers home. I'm alone on the dance-floor and I wonder if rock-bottom is always this mundane and boring, just ugly tears in the club, no different from any other homesick teenager or alcoholic bridesmaid.

That was not when I met Harry. I have to remind myself, because my mind likes to link the events. I met Harry two weeks later off a dating app, when he was, as he wrote to me, "in town for business." I found that unbearably tantalizing and went to dinner with him.

But in my mind, he appears there on the dance-floor. He sees me, he pulls away from the people he's with, he comes up to me and doesn't even say anything, just holds my hand as I cry.

HARRY had to take a meeting halfway through dinner. It was pasta, rigatoni, with some mushroom and corn in it. It had never occurred to me to put corn in pasta.

When Harry's phone rang, he got up very nobly and apologetically, lifted one finger, and gave me a wink. It was so smooth and graceful I didn't even understand what was happening until he was gone from the table.

It was just me and Richard left to keep things moving. I drank my white wine and wondered what to ask, since Richard had already glumly covered his day's activity.

We sat in marble silence for a while, plinking silverware and carefully taking chewy bites. I moved around corn and looked at the chandelier and the wooden shadows of the room.

"Chris," Richard said. I immediately came to attention, like a dog. "Yes?"

"How old was Dad when you were born?"

I squinted as I did the math.

"Uh, he would've been nineteen," I said.

"So my dad's a pedophile."

"No, Richard! Where did you learn the word 'pedophile'?"

"Some old man on the playground told me."

I gave him a solemn, searching look.

"Richard, that did not happen," I said. "That's not funny. Did that happen?"

Richard took a bite of his rigatoni and tried to hide his smirk.

"You're awful. Don't say that around your dad," I said.

Richard burst out laughing. "Pedophile," he repeated.

"Shh!" I said, and started laughing with him.

We smiled, looked down at our plates, and were quiet again.

THAT night I blew Harry in bed, one lamp on, and swallowed like a good little slut. I felt the pleasure of rote learning, the same pride as having performed a violin concerto from memory.

Harry was still breathing hard when he turned off the lamp. I let him gather himself in the darkness.

"Harry," I said. "I don't really like that school Richard goes to."

Harry stroked my hair, the back of my neck, massaged at the soreness. A minute before, he had been shoving it into his cock.

"I know," he said. "I talked to them about that teacher. I took care of all that."

"Really?"

"I know it was bothering you. And you were right."

I was touched, even though I didn't believe him.

"I appreciate it," I said. "Even beyond that, though—"

"It's a good place," Harry said. "It did me a lot of good as a kid. I think it'll do Richard a lot of good too."

"Yeah" I said. "Maybe he'll grow up to be a pedophile like you."

Harry tugged at my hair.

"You're a very sick person," he said with love.

I WAS in an attic, the roof was falling in on me, but I woke up before I could suffocate. Everything was dark. Harry was asleep. I wasn't touching him, and suddenly understood how titanically large the bed was.

I did two rolls over toward the edge and grabbed my phone to check the time. It was 3:28, and I had a notification.

HOW DOES YOUR FOUNTAIN BURBLE?

It was one of Nina's newsletters. I opened it as a fan rotated in the far corner of the bedroom, whooshing like an empty laundry machine. There was a comfortable, early morning cold occupying the room. I shivered and blinked my eyes, trying to adjust to my screen's brightness.

> *most people want fountains that work and ARE crystal clear*
> *like the basins of Antiquity*
> *aahryrrlkkdfkjkkje&%^!!!!!! Indent*

There was a blinking gif of a cat drinking from a pool, but it was distorted, scrambled. The lines vibrated and moved like falling matchsticks.

> *In the end will you be happy with ANYTHING less than*
> **A 100 Percent Working AUTHENTICALLY SOURCED WATER PROVIDER???**
> *&#aajupwerbgoignogu8***

Something got caught in the fan, went click-click-click-click, dislodged itself.

The house was empty again.

I put on my shorts and shoes and didn't let myself look in the mirror.

I started running through the neighborhood, turned the opposite way as last time, and gawked at the ivy and gables and enormous windows.

I was feeling good for the first ten minutes, and then the itch started again, growing redder and redder until it was kissing the inside of my groin and chafing the back of my ass.

I prayed for a nearby meat hook, where I could be hung upside down and have the flesh of my legs removed with scissors.

I was picturing the blood dripping down when I noticed I was in front of a very large lawn, filled with about ten reclining women in lawn chairs. The Chapel Hill breastfeeding mothers, I realized.

They were all looking at me.

"Hi," I said, panting. "I'm so sorry. I'm interrupting mommy group."

They all had books and guides and manuals on their laps, and tall colorful drinks in cupholders. They looked happy and distant.

"It's okay," one mother said. "Take your time."

They all watched me as I scratched at my legs and breathed hard and tried not to moan.

It was 8:30 again.

"Richard," I said. "I'll tuck you in."

He looked at the floor. "Okay."

I pulled up his blanket to his chin and turned off the light. I stood in the darkness.

"Are you going to wait there?" Richard said after a while.

"Oh," I said. "Sorry. Wanted to be sure you were okay."

"I'm fine," he said.

I told Harry I was worried about Richard later that night. He was in a good mood because some business deal with a partner in Virginia had been secured or something.

"He's so quiet," I said. "He never talks about anything. His interests, his life."

"He's just depressed because those Superman comics he ordered haven't come yet," Harry said. The maid had fucked his ties up by mixing the colors, so he was busy re-organizing the whole drawer.

"Really," I said. "Can third-graders be depressed?"

"It'll pass," Harry said. "Everything passes."

"You sound like a proctologist," I said.

"Ha ha," Harry said in a droning voice, to let me know I wasn't funny.

AT the coffee shop, I asked about depression in children.

"Oh, yes," Nina said. "I was basically suicidal in elementary school. Except I didn't realize it. Couldn't even process my emotions enough to get to that."

"So should I be worried about Richard?"

"I don't know," Nina said. "I gave the fucking kid up for a reason."

I nodded and drank my berry tea.

"Do you ever want to do cocaine, like the really rotten type, that's cut with cleaning chemicals?" I said.

"No," she said. "I'm addicted to sex. Are you going to relapse?"

I thought about it.

"No," I said. "I don't have numbers for dealers in this city."

"Like that's ever stopped a person."

"How's the fountain business? Are they selling?"

"Fountains?" she said, alarmed. "What?"

"Your email. About the fountains."

"Oh, the email," she said. "That email was a mistake. I'm working out the kinks."

"I can't run anymore," I said.

"I always hated it," Nina said, and I wasn't sure what either of us were saying.

I'M up in Edenton, North Carolina, outside the Methodist church, and everybody's wearing their best suits and all I can think is *oh my god, none of them are getting married and they still have nicer tuxes than me.*

I'm learning that you can get seasick just by living too close to the water for too long, when you are also trying cake samples and meeting new relatives with old money and thinking about how guiltily relieved you are that none of your friends can afford to fly out for the wedding, because as sure as the moon pulls in the tide, wherever they are, they will be addled messes of drugs and drink and misunderstood debauchery and have to be escorted out and set to sea.

I'm sure that no other twenty-four-year-old has ever been in a more alien situation, am sure that there is some unspoken rule that says twenty-four-year-olds are not allowed to be married in a manner that is taken so seriously and contains so many floral arrangements. It should not be legal. They should only be able to participate in weddings forced by broken condoms or officiated by Mormon churches.

I should not be here, as I'm walking down the aisle with my brother, as I'm watching Harry recite vows he had his secretary write, as Richard, so tall for six, shuffles up, bears that ring like a trooper, as I accidentally slip Harry too much tongue during our first married kiss, as I down three glasses of Prosecco and immediately realize I need to stop, as Harry's best friend, who I've never met, gives a speech about how *industrious* he is, which, in my mind, is a strange thing to emphasize on a day that's supposed to be devoted to the idea of love, as everyone dances and slaps my back and asks which way to the bar and then leaves.

Harry takes viagra in the hotel room. I don't cum. Outside, the sea is loud and unceasing.

On Thursday, we went to a dinner party. It was interesting to be inside a different enormous house. North Carolina manses contained such a dignified, sacred feeling, like they all had been consecrated.

Harry led me through it, down long staircases and into wine cellars and to the outdoor area piled high with red slabs of stones, soon to be used for an outdoor fireplace.

"Everybody I know wants to build a pizza oven" Harry said, "and then they use it once and burn the pizza and never touch it again."

"But talk about it at every party," I said.

"You know how it is," he said, then kissed me. He sucked on my bottom lip, like we were two horny college students in a club, and I was surprised at how hard it made me. I couldn't remember the last time he had been so puerile and undignified with me in a public setting.

I leaned forward for more, but Harry pulled away and patted my dick.

"That's all you get," he said, and kissed my nose. "C'mon, mister."

Harry introduced me to Kelvin, who owned the house and wore two wristwatches on his left hand.

"Cool," I said. "Which one does holograms?"

"He's so funny," Kelvin said to Harry. "Harry always says you're funny."

Like a jinx, I was unfunny the rest of the night. I wandered around as Harry talked to his work buddies and tried to join in on their conversations, but quickly realized I had nothing witty to say about stocks.

I got a grapefruit paloma from the for-hire bartender, then sulked outside by the unbuilt pizza oven and waited for dinner. I wished for the warmth of Los Angeles at night, but could only conjure up a cold wind instead. I wished I was still being kissed.

I crossed my arms to get warm and saw a tall, beaky woman in a swishing lavender dress come outside. She opened her purse and untangled a breast pump from a mess of scrunchies.

She looked up and saw me.

"Pump and dump night," she said.

"Every night, girl," I said in my faggiest voice, so she'd know it was safe to pull out her breasts in front of me.

She laughed and sat next to me and, sure enough, removed one breast from her dress and attached the pump to it.

"I know you," she said.

"Yeah. I think we live in the same neighborhood. I ran by your mom group the other day."

"That's right. Is your rash better?" It was a manual pump she was working, and I watched little dribbles of milk fall into the plastic like the first drops of rain in a drought. A sudden, vicious maternal wanting clawed at me.

"Can't figure it out," I said. "It happens whenever I run now."

"Awful. Especially since I'm sure that's such an escape for you."

That wasn't how I viewed it. I wondered if I wasn't thinking about escape as often as I should.

Harry poked his head outside, saw me, saw the woman's breasts, then cheekily covered his eyes.

"Time for dinner, whenever you've finished this illicit affair," he said.

"Ha ha," I said in a droning voice, like he did when I wasn't funny. Harry smiled, but narrowed his eyes as he went back inside.

I turned to the woman. "Do you—excuse, me what's your name?"

"Leandra," she said.

"Do you have coke, Leandra?"

She froze, let those tiny drops of milk patter into the bottle.

"No, I do not," she said. "I think we should head to dinner."

I SAT at the far end of a great oak table, next to Harry. There were about twenty people gathered, waitstaff distributing cuts of roast and fragrant asparagus. The ceiling was glass, and the moon and stars were shining hard. The light reflected off both of Kelvin's watches and kept getting in my eyes.

"What are you swatting at?" Harry said. He turned to the man on his other side, Manny or Matthew. "The hardest part, and you know this—"

"—time away from wife and kids," Manny/Matthew nodded.

"Exactly," Harry said. "And the wife can get pretty upset."

He nudged me in the side like a 40s comedy bit, too hard. I didn't feel like playing along, so I just blinked neutrally and said nothing.

Manny/Matt laughed anyway and kept on talking.

"Your boy is how old now? I remember him coming into the office—"

"Three years ago! When he was just five. He's eight already. In the third grade down at Harris Junior—"

"Great school," Manny/Matt said. "Eight. Ridiculous."

"Is your name Manny or Matthew?" I said.

He looked confused. "I'm Brian."

"This is Brian," Harry said.

"Sorry," I said. "Do your kids go to Harris?"

Brian shook his head. "No, we're not in the area, otherwise—"

"Does anybody know what they're doing down there?"

"Excuse me?" Brian said.

"Chris," Harry said, then to Brian, "Here goes the wife."

"Don't call me your wife," I said.

Harry gripped his fork tight. He pressed his shoe down on mine, kept it heavy there.

"Really," I said. "Harry doesn't care. He has no idea what's going on with Richard. Maybe you're the same with your kids."

"I think that's probably quite unfair," Brian said.

"I would say it's exceptionally unfair," Harry said, and pressed his foot down harder. He was looking around the table, making sure no one else was paying attention to us.

"I don't think so. I mean, I barely have a fucking clue what's running through Richard's mind, and I'm with him a lot more than Harry is."

"Not true."

"Okay, say whatever you want at this dinner party."

Brian opened his mouth, ready to say something, but Harry leapt in before he could.

"You have been here—you have been around him for barely four years," he said, his fork quivering in his hand. "You are a tourist in Richard's life."

I could smell the blood from the roast, and the urine-y asparagus that was now limp on my plate. Everything inside of me was roaring.

"No, that's wrong," I said. "I'm the one who sits with him at the table when you have to go yell on the phone. I'm the one who puts him to bed—"

"Two years," Harry said. Brian was softly scratching at the table in discomfort, eyes downward. "Two years we've been married and Richard still doesn't call you 'dad.' Says just about fucking everything you need to know."

"You used to be so sweet," I said, and reached over Harry to tap on Brian's plate with my oily knife. "Did he ever tell you how we met? I was in this gross club in Los Angeles, can you believe that, on some really bad cocaine that actually had me crying, and he came over—"

"That's not how we met," Harry said. "I wasn't there."

I pulled my foot out from underneath his. "Can't you ever just go along with it? Jesus Christ, it makes you look good."

He didn't say anything. I looked back down at the asparagus wasting away on my plate. I swallowed and drew lines in the condensation of my water glass.

At the other end of the table, Leandra was laughing vibrantly, the men next to her smiling. Their meals were cut up perfectly, and Leandra popped in the daintiest piece of roast with expert precision before swallowing and starting on another joke.

ALOE PLANTS

what's wrong with them?

d   indent ancing Flower sdhfaiughgojsdfou^@chris.tevis@lynndubois

They're NOT a orchid!

click the link to hear a CLIENT signing to their new favorite plant1 auegieriwiroewijnsasghhghjagkjgaskjg;h;akj

Pre-order

SOON TO BE AVAILABLE!

I TEXTED Nina but she didn't respond. That got me worried. Her emails seemed to be getting more and more scattered. I decided to go to a different coffee shop, farther away from Harry's neighborhood. The barista was more stressed than the one at our usual place. His undershirt was crumpled and streaked white with deodorant stains.

"Hi," I said. "Do you have elderberry or blackberry tea?"

I took my drink and moved toward the window table, jostling past a few jittery looking customers, and had to stop and make sure I was right, because Mr. Byrie, Richard's teacher, was sitting alone at a table with two empty coffee cups.

"Mr. Byrie?" I said. I had been standing there too long to get away without saying something. "Isn't it a school day?"

He swiveled, his chair dragging against the floor, saw who it was, and rubbed at the sides of his glasses.

"For employed teachers," he said, "sure."

"Oh." I looked around the coffee shop, felt some sweat beading on my back. "Did you quit, or…"

"Fired," Mr. Byrie said. "I was fired. Your husband had a productive phone call with the principal."

"Oh," I said again. "I'm surprised that he called. And it was about…?"

"Do you know why I didn't let your son go the bathroom?"

"I mean—"

"He's in there masturbating. Constantly. Other kids have seen." Mr. Byrie grabbed one of his coffee cups, seeming to forget it was empty. "I don't know if anybody's talked to him about it at home, or if he can't find time to do it there, but after about the tenth bathroom visit of the day, I decided maybe it wasn't so good to accommodate that urge."

I tried to swallow in an inconspicuous way. "Shouldn't you have called Harry? Isn't there protocol?"

"Protocol? For explaining to your nightmare of a husband that his child is a pervert?"

I was surprised how differently he talked outside of school.

"So…there isn't," I said.

Mr. Byrie gave me the coldest shark eyes I'd ever seen.

"I'm really sorry," I said. "I'm sure you'll find another gig."

"*Gig?*"

I decided it would be best to take my tea to go.

No one talked at dinner. I didn't eat. It was a light, spring-y soup with chicken and lots of green onions, and it was still too much for me.

"Why don't you go tuck Richard in?" Harry said. "I know how important it is to you."

After I pulled up his sheets, I said to Richard, "Why didn't you tell me that Mr. Byrie left?"

"I don't know," Richard said. "You didn't seem to like him."

"Well, I thought he wasn't treating you very nicely."

Richard didn't say anything.

"I heard you go to the bathroom a lot at school."

He became even more still.

"It's okay," I said. "But maybe you can save that stuff for later. Times like now. After I leave the room."

Richard pulled the sheets away from his chin, disgruntled. "Chris," he said, "what are you even talking about?"

How was I supposed to know? How was I supposed to know how to teach an uncool eight-year-old about jacking off? How was I any older, any wiser than him? In the scale of years and time and everything else, I was closer to him than my own husband.

"Richard," I said, "I'm just glad you've figured out what makes you happy."

I WAITED in bed in my underwear, thinking maybe I should use my body in some sexual way to ward of the growing, edgy feeling of horror and shame that was moving through me. Harry was in his office, talking on the phone, so I killed time by pulling off my fingernails, and soon Harry was off the phone but still in his office, and then an hour had passed, and then two, and I understood he would not be entering the room as long as the lights were on and I was awake.

I got up and put on one of my old shirts and a pair of tight jeans. I walked right past the closed door of Harry's office and called an Uber.

It was a buzzing pre-summer night. The people we drove by seemed animated with an intense, maniacal energy, like tarantists, as they headed to the bars.

"Here is good," I said when we reached one of the only nightclubs in town.

The line was long but that didn't matter to me. In half an hour the bouncer let me in, and I was immediately overwhelmed by the music and the lights. I felt like a dirty, dog-tagged veteran, even though I was younger than many of the people there.

Everyone seemed cleaner-cut than they were in my days in LA, more peppy and colorful and less scraggly. I wasn't sure who was likeliest to have coke; my navigation system had been short-circuited by marriage. Finally, I decided that the bathroom was the best place to start.

There was one group of shrieking guys at the sinks. I asked them if they had any coke I could pilfer.

"*Pilfer?*" they said, laughing, and then walked out.

I washed my hands after they were gone, even though they were clean. I made the mistake of looking at myself in the mirror.

"You are not ugly," I said, but I couldn't find any evidence to support that. Two lanky men came out of the stall, wiping their mouths and hair.

"Please," I said. "Do you have any coke?"

They had about a quarter of a baggie they poured out into five lines. I got to work, watching my reflection in the watery, black bathroom counter.

Did I want to cry?

I couldn't tell. My breath was rising, catching in my throat, the last clicks before a roller coaster falls.

My phone dinged.

> **Unfortunately ART doesn't come to You**
> *Until*
> *dasfkjNOW !*

I wiped at my nose and started typing a reply to Nina's email.

> **NINA**
> *I am*
> *high ON cocaine…heard of IT!!!! &&&&&*
> *I am going to RUN AWAY and never think about*
> *Small bodies*
> *Indent   AGAIN*

I left the bathroom and got lost in the crowd of bodies. I stood there as people danced around me, preparing myself for last call, preparing to find my bus card and my debit card and pull out enough money to make it to a hotel in Tennessee.

My phone dinged with another email from Nina.

Chris, it said, and there were no typos or strange capitalizations or faulty URLs. The message was clearheaded and perfect.

Chris, it said.

Do not worry. I am coming with you.
I started to cry.

WE'RE down at a zoo, and there's a class of children on a field trip being led by an enthusiastic woman in a safari hat. I'm thinking about the way hyenas laugh and wondering how the zookeepers clean all that water in the enormous fish tanks, and I can smell tufts of cotton candy and brine and shitty mud and the melting soles of tennis shoes, leaving behind bits of sticky rubber like gum. It's too hot out, isn't that how it always is, and I feel myself burning up, burning up with the kind of fresh, athletic sunburn I haven't felt since my days doing track in middle school.

I am not thinking about anything beyond this. I have never heard of sex, I have never done drugs, I don't know what a wedding is or where babies come from. What's in front of me is in front of me. All my pipes have been cleared with No-Rust-Stuff. I can feel myself edging toward something that is new to me, beyond me, a release that doesn't have to do with my hands or my legs or the way I talk. It's like laughter, it's like rain, it's like a nursing mother: it's happening to me, it's happening to me, oh my god, it's finally coming

Nancy Naomi Carlson

WE WEREN'T SO JEWISH THEN

Dangling our faith on a golden chain,
we gave our children Old Testament
names like Matthew and Aaron and Ruth
to honor the family dead
piling up faster by year—

a whirlwind of covered mirrors, black
ribbons, and yahrzeit candles burning
in glass—and words like *brucha* and *yizkor*
at graveside prayer, layering stone
upon stone like ancient tropes,

but still we wedded outside the tribe,
drawn to men who'd never donned a skullcap,
yet stomped on glass, timid shards
in their soles, to prove their accepting love—
our mothers, defied, turned away and closed

their eyes each Shabbat, gathering
candlelight in their hands—a vigil
to combat the dark they feared
we'd brought upon ourselves—more dreadful
than any epithet sprayed on our walls.

DOG STAR

For Gigi, on the first anniversary of her dying

For loyalty's sake let's grant her kind
her due, as even in biblical Egypt
no dogs barked when the Israelites fled.
Talmudic scholars might lend her
the animal soul—the *nefesh*—let it reside
in her blood, though they'd deny her
that divine spark—the *neshama*—
that would allow her to ponder the difference.

Did you know that the ancient Egyptians
convinced themselves that the heart
housed the so-called human soul,
and death sealed one's fate by weight—
heart versus feather—the lighter the better—
though pharaohs got a free pass to ascend?

Do the best dogs get to become one
with Sirius—the size of two suns
and twenty-five times more luminous,
whose dogged fetch and return
ancient astronomers tracked *per annum*
each time the Nile overran its banks?

And now in these Days of Awe of early fall,
Sirius sits low in the nighttime sky.
We Jews scrub out our sins, like stains,
and remember our dead—human or beast.

After the shofar sounds one last time,
the Book of Life will be sealed for the year,
and we'll look to the sky for that first star
to signal the end of Yom Kippur's fast,
when the first bite of food to breach our lips
tastes sweetest after a day of going without,
and a star might wag its diaphanous tail
even in the darkest of nights.
What after all is a soul?

Caleb Berer

AN INTERVIEW WITH WILHELM SITZ

Wilhelm Sitz, whose story "Release" appears in this issue of the magazine, writes mostly at a white desk in his bedroom. The desk, as Wilhelm tells me, is "not extremely large". Its surface and its immediate surroundings are crowded with life's essentials: wallet, keys, tissues, good books, "tiny babies and frog necklaces" from the sidewalk, "some unframed pictures, drawings, old visitor passes, crew tags for when I pretended to work at the Hollywood Bowl". There are other things as well. On the wall there is a poster for House on Haunted Hill, *wherein Vincent Price is "always unhappily looking down." This was all a little like hearing a description of the neighborhood I grew up in, offered by another person who grew up in the same neighborhood, but with a slightly different view. My desk is extremely large, and not white, but black. Still it is crowded—there are drawings, books, unframed photos, things I found on the pavement, happy recollections of various deceptions. And I am, as I write this, looking up at, and being looked down on, by a photo of a frowning man, though he is not Vincent Price. We tend, as Wilhelm says, to keep our memories "close and in-sight". In the conversation that follows, which has been edited for length and clarity, we discuss the presence of the past, the drive "to become formally and structurally unbound", and the libidinous delight to be found in shit-talking other people's art—respectfully, of course.*

INTERVIEWER

How did this story begin for you? With an image, a phrase, the first line? More generally, do your stories tend to originate in similar ways?

WILHELM SITZ

I started this piece after I saw some parents/Internet people on

Twitter sharing their stories about teachers not letting kids go to the bathroom during class—justified outrage, I think. But I enjoy a little controversy in my work and I thought about possible reasonings that went beyond pure discipline. Kids are great but also very weird, and so the idea of poor compulsive masturbating Richard came to my head. I liked the idea of writing a domestic story and thought this incident would be a good starting point for some great unraveling. From there, I threw in all my generalized anxieties and complicated feelings about fatherhood as a gay man, and then it was off to the races. This was a fun and relatively easy story for me to write—most of the time I give up halfway through, restart, then begin the cycle all over again. But my stories generally always come from some small things like that—something I witness in person, see online, or some thought that bubbles up while I'm walking and not thinking about much else.

INTERVIEWER

I liked your first sentence—"There was trouble at the school." It immediately puts us in a place, and a predicament, yet it leaves the door open, so to speak. We could go to a lot of places, hit lot of notes, and we do. Was this always the first line? More generally, do your first lines tend to remain the same—minor edits notwithstanding—in the course of drafting, or is it common for them to change entirely? Are there any opening lines from other writers that have really stuck with you?

WILHELM SITZ

Thank you. That was always the first line. I'm a big proponent of having a distinct and memorable sentence to start things off. I like to show readers immediately where we're going, then try to subvert that later on. Because of that, I really need to get that first sentence right before I dig into a story, so what I have drafted usually stays.

Lorrie Moore is amazing at opening lines that instantly feel loaded with meaning without trying too hard. Her first sentences in *Self-Help* are especially masterful.

INTERVIEWER

I was struck by the phrase "strange, electric discharges." The words refer to Chris's hope that "One day, Richard's brain would spark in the right part of the cortex", and he would be "overcome" with love, or at least guilt, but Chris's visceral memories of cocaine—not to mention the high itself—are also certainly a strange, electric discharge; in a manner of speaking, so are Nina's incomprehensible 3 AM emails; perhaps even Richard's compulsive masturbation. Do you see this as a major motif in the story? How did it first appear, and how did it grow?

WILHELM SITZ

That was unintentional, or unconscious, but it does seem to be a bigger theme now that you bring it up. I think most of us writers have brains short-circuiting in a variety of weird and maybe malignant ways—I am constantly questioning the things I do and trying to track down how they can be the result of a little spark inside me. I first wrote that line because, while it's true to some extent, it's also a desperate excuse. Chris is so lost at sea that the only way he can hope for love or acceptance is through somebody else's brain glitch. So I guess that idea, of how governed we are not only by our own horrible thoughts but the ones of the people around us, started coming out more in other characters until, as you say, it became a kind of motif.

INTERVIEWER

Throughout the story, increasingly agitated with his "perfect life", which is of course not so perfect, Chris gravitates towards the Chapel Hill breastfeeders. I was particularly drawn to the scene—funny, and wrenching—where he asks Leandra if she has any coke. It seemed to represent a wonderfully complex confluence of desires and perceptions. Could you unpack that dynamic a little? Why is Chris so drawn to these women? What do they represent for him? And, in the Leandra scene, are we witnessing a deliberate act of self-sabotage, and alienation? Or is this an attempt to connect?

WILHELM SITZ

Leandra and the gorgeous Chapel Hill breastfeeders are where all of Chris' misplaced hopes go. He sees these women as wives who've figured out exactly what their station is and how to navigate it. They're "real" mothers, with kids who came from their bodies and, presumably, love them unconditionally. They aren't scared or lost in this world of wealth like Chris is. They've reached domestic transcendence. Chris especially fixates on the breast-feeding because, to him, it's something so natural, loving, and nourishing which he will never be capable of. As a gay man, he knows he will never be able to have a child in this way, even as he's reduced to Harry's "wife." I think the scene with Leandra at the dinner party is a mixture of insane hope, deliberate self-sabotage, and learned behaviors. He wants acceptance so badly, but doesn't know how to assimilate—back in LA, I imagine he mostly connected with people through drugs and alcohol. But this isn't his LA. He knows that, but hopes that Leandra is some magic fluke who will shatter his own illusions about North Carolina and this new world around him.

INTERVIEWER

Building on that question: what is it that attracts Nina and Chris to one another? Of course there's the Harry/Richard connection, but what do you see as being at the very center of their relationship? And what is the reader to make of Nina's final email, "clearheaded and perfect", promising to run away with Chris?

WILHELM SITZ

I think Nina and Chris are, to some extent, friends by default. They're caught in the stuffy languor of their lives and using each other to try to figure themselves out. At first, I think they're only talking at each other—depending on your outlook on the ending, maybe they still are. But I think a switch happens, when they both realize that they are not the people they've been pretending they are. They're trapped in something beyond them. When Nina realizes this—spurred by Chris' relapse—she escapes her email purgatory and is finally able to say: we can escape this.

Maybe it's short-sighted, but I do believe it's the first time both of them finally take their lives into their own hands.

INTERVIEWER

The flashbacks in the story, which have to do with Chris's former (or not-so-former) relationship with cocaine and the single-life, occur in present tense, as the rest of the story occurs in past. I have my own theories, thematically speaking, for why that might be, but I'm curious to know if you had a conscious rationale for that choice. More broadly, how do formal and structural decisions like that tend to work their way into your composition? Are these planned moves, spontaneous, little bit of both?

WILHELM SITZ

In every story I write, I'm looking for some moment to become formally and structurally unbound. So, a kind of planned spontaneity, or one that I hope to find. I switched to present-tense flashbacks here when I was feeling stuck, and it immediately made the way clear. There's a variety of reasons why I changed tense (and am happy that you have your own theories): firstly, I liked the idea of making a flashback feel more immediate and vivid than the actual present, because that's exactly how Chris feels about his life at this point. The past is more real and, in a way, still happening to him. I also like the idea that he's reciting these memories out loud to somebody—maybe Nina. And lastly, I wanted the ending to feel ambiguous and out-of-time. Maybe Chris has snapped into the realness of his life and is really seeing, as he says, that what's in front of him is in front of him. Whether that's through his escape with Nina, or with Harry and Richard who he's returned to, I'm not sure (but have a guess). Or maybe he's still caught in the slipstream of the past and this is just another memory giving him hope that he can achieve some great revelation, or confirmation that he never will.

INTERVIEWER

This is a story that doesn't shy away from big themes: class, sexual orientation, addiction, parenting, and (naturally) compulsive masturbation. Big, nationally pertinent themes. Yet it handles the subject matter nimbly; it's never didactic. It's very funny. I've heard writers talk about constantly correcting, or balancing out these questions of tone, as they revise, and I'm curious to know what your revision process looks like. Does the basic tone and shape appear in the first draft, or do things change drastically? Or does it depend on the story?

WILHELM SITZ

Tone is where I feel most confident as a writer. I am insecure and whiny about a million other things, but when I start writing a story, I have a very good handle on the tone I want to achieve. Or, if I find that I'm not achieving it, I abandon the story like a coward. So maybe it's not that I'm across-the-board good at it, but I have hit the mark enough times for me to believe that there's some capability there. In any case, I'm glad you thought it wasn't didactic, which is one of my big fears as a writer. I don't like prescriptive things, and even with the most gut-wrenching sorrow—my preferred subject matter—I need a little bit of humor.

This may sound conceited, but actually it's lazy: I don't do huge revisions. I will start and stop a story a million times over, but once I finish a story, I usually only go back to fiddle with paragraphs, cut unnecessary scenes/sentences, and try to make everything shine. I don't often do major rehauls. Again, I think that's partly laziness but also partly because I'm in revision mode as soon as I write the first sentence. I need a good scaffolding of words to build off.

INTERVIEWER

In your unofficial bio, you mentioned growing up in rural Oregon, working as a ranch-hand, drag queen, and muralist's assistant. Can I ask what the best and/or worst day jobs you've ever had were? How has writing fit into your working life? Do you have an MFA, or do you consider yourself more self-taught? Do you have any advice for young writers out there, trying to pay the bills while cultivating a so-called literary life?

WILHELM SITZ

My best day-job, which was only a week in college, was working as a receptionist for a Batman virtual-reality game. My professor hired me as a ditzy secretary character to check people in and prime them for the experience. I got to concoct a beautiful backstory for this idiot secretary, dole it out in pieces to different guests, and play Enya on a loop all day.

As far as worst jobs, dishwashing sucked. I lost my fingerprints for a few months from the water and heat. I'm a caregiver now, which has been a good, steady job that gives me time to write. It's hard: I need these jobs and experiences to feel like I have something to write about (not to mention finance my life), but it's a struggle to find the time and energy to actually do that writing. Usually, I end up working in fits and starts and sporadic bursts. The idea of a routine appeals to me but I haven't been able to nail one down yet. As far as schooling—I don't have an MFA, but I do have a BFA in Screenwriting from USC. I wrote prose as a kid, then fell in love with the idea of writing TV, then graduated college and couldn't get a job, and returned to prose through a writers' group that one of my professors was a part of. (The same professor who hired me as the receptionist, in fact. Maureen is the best.) That screenwriting experience helped hone my prose writing, and when I get tired of one, I go back to the other.

For advice, I don't have a lot. Find jobs with lots of downtime. Try to live in areas with other young artists who also feel lost. Experience as much strangeness as you can. Make different kinds of art. For birthdays and Christmas, ask for subscriptions to literary journals. (Like the *Potomac Review*!) Try to engage with art as much as you can, and try to make it good art. Although, I never feel more literary than when I encounter something I despise and can shit-talk it with my friends. Respectfully.

INTERVIEWER

Who are the writers that are really exciting to you right now? We could be talking dead, contemporary, whatever you'd like.

WILHELM SITZ

This story was heavily influenced by Lorrie Moore, who I mentioned before and love. Lately, I'm ecstatic about Helen DeWitt and Kathy Acker (RIP), whose *The Last Samurai* and *Blood and Guts in High School* blew my mind in surprisingly similar ways. I just read amazing stories by Addie Citchens and Kate Riley in the winter issue of *The Paris Review* and promptly ordered Riley's new book, *Miriam*. And Jennifer Egan, Annie Proulx, Kelly Link, and Derek McCormack are perennial favorites.

INTERVIEWER

Do you have any projects you're excited about at the moment? Anything you'd like our readers to know about?

WILHELM SITZ

I'm in a bit of a flux state right now—working on a bunch of stories I can't nail down and desperately trying to figure out how to write a novel. Me and my friend Emily are currently making a zine, so if there are any readers in Los Angeles, stay tuned for the launch and maybe even a release party with cake.

***

Wilhelm Sitz is a writer from rural Oregon. Now, he lives in Los Angeles. His work has appeared or is forthcoming in Southeast Review, Sycamore Review, *and* Sundog Lit.

──────────── Contributors ────────────

LINETTE MARIE ALLEN, winner of the 2021 Kay Murphy Prize for Poetry, holds an MFA in Creative Writing and the Publishing Arts from the University of Baltimore. A Turner Fellow, she has published work in *Pleiades, Gulf Coast, Prairie Schooner*, and elsewhere. Her writing was twice nominated for the Best of the Net Awards and has been set to music by composers at The Peabody Institute. She is a native of Washington, DC.

NANCY NAOMI CARLSON, winner of the 2022 Oxford-Weidenfeld Translation Prize, twice an NEA translation grant recipient, and the Translations Editor for On the Seawall, has published thirteen titles (four non-translated). *An Infusion of Violets* (Seagull, 2019), her second full-length poetry collection, was called "new & noteworthy" by *The New York Times*. *Piano in the Dark* is forthcoming from Seagull Books next month.

MATT COLBURN will begin his MFA in Fiction at NYU Fall 2023. He holds an MA in English from Brown University and a BA in English from Kenyon College. He has taught English at the community college level since 2014. He earned the 2018 University of the District of Columbia Community College Outstanding Adjunct Faculty of the Year Award and a 2018-2019 Montgomery College Outstanding Part-time Faculty Award. He posts educational videos to his YouTube channel, youtube.com/ColburnClassroom. • Twitter: @colburnclassrm • Website: colburnclassroom.com.

LIGHTSEY DARST is a writer, mother, and worker living in Durham, NC. *The Heiress/Ghost Acres* is forthcoming from Coffee House Press in spring 2023.

CHRISTINA DAUB is a Pushcart Prize nominated poet, whose work has appeared in many literary journals and anthologies. The founder

CONTRIBUTORS

of *The Plum Review*, she has taught poetry and creative writing in the English Department at George Washington University and in both the Maryland and Virginia Poets-in-the-Schools programs, as well as to adults for many years at The Writer's Center. Her work has been translated into Russian, German and Italian.

SARA RIES DZIEKONSKI holds an MFA in poetry from Chatham University. Her first book, *Come In, We're Open*, won the 2009 Stevens Poetry Manuscript Competition. Her chapbooks include *Snow Angels on the Living Room Floor* (Finishing Line Press 2018) and *Marrying Maracuyá* (Main Street Rag 2021), which won the Cathy Smith Bowers Chapbook Competition. Her poems have appeared in *Slipstream, LABOR: Studies in Working-Class History of the Americas, Cathexis Northwest Press, The Buffalo News, Cordella Magazine, 2River View*, among others. She is the co-founder of Poetry Midwives Editing Services.

ALEXANDER ETHERIDGE has been developing his poems and translations since 1998. His poems have been featured in *The Potomac Review, Scissors and Spackle, Ink Sac, Cerasus Journal, The Cafe Review, The Madrigal, Abridged Magazine, Susurrus Magazine, The Journal, Roi Faineant Press*, and many others. He was the winner of the Struck Match Poetry Prize in 1999, and a finalist for the Kingdoms in the Wild Poetry Prize in 2022. He is the author of two forthcoming collections, *God Said Fire*, and *Snowfire and Home*.

LEILA FARJAMI is a poet, literary translator, and psychotherapist. In addition to publishing seven poetry books in Persian, her work has appeared in *Nimrod Journal*; was published by Tupelo Press for their 30/30 Project; and has been translated into Swedish, Arabic, Turkish, and French. Leila has appeared in poetry readings and on Persian TV and radio interviews about her poetry. She studies poetry with Rachel Kann, enjoys translating sacred poetry by Rumi into English, and has translated a comprehensive volume of Sylvia Plath's poetry into Persian.

ANDY FOGLE is the author of *Across from Now* and seven chapbooks of poetry, including the forthcoming chapbook *Arc & Seam: Poems of Farouk Goweda*, co-translated with Walid Abdallah. He's from Virginia Beach and the DC area, and now lives with his family in upstate NY, teaching high school. He was the recipient of a 2021 Individual Artist Grant from Saratoga Arts to write poems related to abolitionist John Brown. Music, collage, and poetry can be found at fogle.bandcamp.com.

TONI HOLLAND's awards include a student Fulbright Fellowship at the University of Alberta, residency at The Millay Colony for the Arts, two at The Vermont Studio Center; she's been a Tumbleweed in Shakespeare and Company. Her work has appeared in *Illya's Honey, Jelly Bucket, Tau, Rip Rap*, and *Poetry International: Cinepoetry, New Letters*, and *Solstice Literary Magazine*.

NATALIE HOMER's recent poetry has been published in *Puerto del Sol, American Literary Review, Four Way Review, Ruminate, Sou'wester*, and others. She received an MFA from West Virginia University and lives in southwestern Pennsylvania. Her first collection, *Under the Broom Tree*, is forthcoming from Autumn House Press.

MEGAN HOWELL is a DC-based freelance writer. She earned her MFA in Fiction from the University of Maryland in College Park, winning both the Jack Salamanca Thesis Award and the Kwiatek Fellowship. Her work has appeared in *McSweeney's, The Nashville Review* and *The Establishment*, among other publications.

SIMON HOWELLS was born in Wales in 1971.

JOHN HYLAND's poems have recently appeared in *Valparaiso Poetry Review, Laurel Review, Atlanta Review*, and *Harvard Review*. He teaches at Berkshire School.

DUSTIN KING would always rather be sneaking a bottle of wine into a movie theater. When nothing good is playing, he teaches Spanish in

Richmond, Virgnia. His poems appear in *Autofocus Lit, South Broadway Ghost Society, Blood and Bourbon, Ligeia,* and other journals.

BETH KONKOSKI is a writer and high school English teacher living in Northern Virginia with her husband and two mostly grown kids. Wandering in the woods and across a page are two of her favorite pastimes. Her work has been published in journals such as: *The American Journal of Poetry, Gargoyle,* and *The Potomac Review.* She has two chapbooks of poetry: *Noticing the Splash* with BoneWorld Press and *Water Shedding* with Finishing Line Press.

YVONNE HIGGINS LEACH is the author of *Another Autumn* (Cherry Grove Collections, 2014). Her poems have been published in *The South Carolina Review, South Dakota Review, Spoon River Review, The Cimarron Review, POEM,* and others. She spent decades balancing a career in communications and public relations, raising a family, and pursuing her love of writing poetry. Her latest passion is working with shelter dogs. She splits her time living on Vashon Island and in Spokane, Washington. For more information, visit yvonnehigginsleach.com.

WHITNEY LEE is Maternal Fetal Medicine physician, former OpEd Public Voices fellow, and veteran. She received her MFA from Vermont College of Fine Arts. Her work has appeared in *The Threepenny Review, Pleiades, Ninth Letter, Booth, Typehouse, Lunch Ticket, The Rumpus, Crack the Spine, Gravel, Numéro Cinq,* and others. She is the recipient of an Illinois Arts Council Agency Literary Award, made the Best American Essays Notable list for 2019 and 2021, and was awarded Pushcart Prize in 2022. She lives in Chicago with her family. Currently, she is working on a memoir.

DEREK MONG is the author of two poetry collections from Saturnalia Books, *Other Romes* (2011) and *The Identity Thief* (2018). His chapbook, *The Ego and the Empiricist* (2017), was a finalist for the Two Sylvias Press Chapbook Prize. An Associate Professor of English at Wabash College, he holds degrees from Stanford, the University of Michigan, and Denison University. His poetry, essays, and translations have appeared widely: the *LA Times*, the *Boston Globe*, the *Kenyon Review*, *Blackbird*, *Crazyhorse*, *Pleiades*, *Verse Daily*, and the *New England Review*. The recipient of awards and fellowships from the University of Louisville, the University of Wisconsin, the *Missouri Review*, and *Willapa Bay AiR*, he lives in Indiana with his family. He and his wife, Anne O. Fisher, received the 2018 Cliff Becker Translation Award for *The Joyous Science: Selected Poems of Maxim Amelin* (White Pine, 2018). He is a contributing editor at *Zócalo Public Square*.

DEREK OTSUJI is the author of *The Kitchen of Small Hours*, winner of the Crab Orchard Review Poetry Series, Open Competition. His recent work has appeared in *32 Poems*, *The Southern Review* and *The Threepenny Review*. New poems are forthcoming in *Cincinnati Review* and *Poetry Northwest*.

SARATH REDDY enjoys writing poetry which explores the world beneath the superficial layers of experience, searching for deeper meaning in his experiences as an Indian-American, as a physician, and as a father. Sarath's poetry has been published in *JAMA*, *Off the Coast*, and *Please see Me*. His work is forthcoming in *Another Chicago Magazine*, *Poetry East*, *Hunger Mountain*, and *Cold Mountain Review*. He lives in Brookline, Massachusetts.

LUKE ROLFES' first book *Flyover Country* won the Georgetown Review Press Short Story Collection Contest, and his second book *Impossible Naked Life* won the Acacia Fiction Prize from Kallisto Gaia Press. His novel *Sleep Lake* is forthcoming from Braddock Avenue Books. He teaches creative writing at Northwest Missouri State University, edits *Laurel Review*, and served as a mentor in the AWP Writer to Writer Program.

PHILIP JAMES SHAW writes, paints, and creates communications on behalf of organizations advancing equity and access in healthcare and education. He lives in Port Townsend, Washington. More about his work can be found at: philipjamesshaw.com.

CONTRIBUTORS

CATHY SHUMAN teaches at Duke University. Her creative nonfiction has appeared in *Under the Gum Tree*. Her work on Victorian literature has been published by Stanford University Press.

WILHELM SITZ is a writer from rural Oregon. Now, he lives in Los Angeles. His work has appeared or is forthcoming in *Southeast Review*, *Sycamore Review*, and *Sundog Lit*.

KATHERINE D. STUTZMAN's stories have appeared in *Bellingham Review, Ascent,* and *Passages North*, among other journals. A graduate of the MFA program at Penn State University, she currently lives, writes, and teaches in Philadelphia. Find her online at: katherinedstutzman.com.

PETER VERTACNIK's work has appeared recently in *32 Poems, The Hopkins Review, Literary Matters* and *THINK*, among others. A finalist for the 2021 Donald Justice Poetry Prize and the 2022 New Criterion Poetry Prize, he currently lives in Gainesville, Florida.

NAOMI WEISS is a creative non-fiction writer and essayist. She was co-author of the 1990s Business Week bestseller *What The IRS Doesn't Want You to Know* (Villard), seven editions, recommended by *The New Yorker, The New York Times,* and *Wall Street Journal. Hedda's Story*, on domestic violence, was a *People Magazine* cover story, for which she appeared on the Oprah Winfrey Show, and A & E's American Justice. Recent work has appeared in *Splice Today, I Come From the World, Montgomery Magazine, Furious Gravity*, an anthology of D.C. Women Writers, *The Book Woman* and Canada's *NIV Magazine*. She is a member of The National Press Club, Member Book and Author Group, Washington, D.C.; the Journalism Institute; the Women's National Book Association, and The Writer's Center, Bethesda, M.D. Website: naomiweiss.net.

CHARLOTTE WYATT earned an MFA at the University of Houston's Creative Writing program, where she was awarded an Inprint

Donald Barthelme Prize for fiction and served as a Fiction Editor for *Gulf Coast*. She has worked for the Napa Valley Writers' Conference since 2016, where she now directs the fiction program. Her work has received support from the NVWC, the Desert Nights, Rising Stars Conference, and the National Parks Service, and can be found in *Gulf Coast, Electric Literature, Joyland*, and others. Charlotte currently lives and works in Las Vegas.

CPSIA information can be obtained
at www.ICGtesting.com
Printed in the USA
BVHW031614030523
663513BV00004B/8